TRACY
BARRETT

ANNA of BYZANTIUM

LAUREL-LEAF
BOOKS

Published by
Dell Laurel-Leaf
an imprint of
Random House Children's Books
a division of Random House, Inc.
1540 Broadway
New York, New York 10036

All quotations of Kassia's poetry are taken from Antonía Tripolitis, editor and translator, Kassia: The Legend, the Woman and Her Work, Garland Library of Medieval Literature, Vol. 84 Series A. New York and London: Garland Publishing, Inc., 1992.

Visit us on the Web! www.randomhouse.com/teens

Educators and librarians, for a variety of teaching tools, visit us at
www.randomhouse.com/teachers

ISBN: 0-440-41536-5
RL: 5.0
Reprinted by arrangement with Delacorte Press
Printed in the United States of America
October 2000
10 9 8 7 6 5 4 3 2 1
OPM

would never have written this book without the help and encouragement of the members of the Green Hills Critique Group. My deepest thanks are due to them to Meghan Ducey for her careful reading of the manuscript, and to my editor, Francoise Bui, for her expert guidance.

Venice

Brundisium

Sardica
(Sofia)

Dyrrhachium

Adriano

Thessalonika

*Aegean
Sea*

Thebes

Corinth

CRETE

BYZANTINE
EMPIRE
under
ALEXIUS I COMNENUS
1081–1118

The COMNENUS and DUCAS FAMILIES

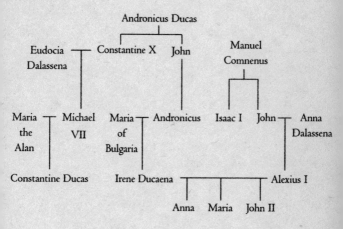

Andronicus Ducas

Eudocia Dalassena ─ Constantine X   John

Manuel Comnenus

Maria the Alan ─ Michael VII   Maria of Bulgaria ─ Andronicus   Isaac I   John ─ Anna Dalassena

Constantine Ducas   Irene Ducaena ─ Alexius I

Anna   Maria   John II

EMPERORS	RULED
Isaac I Comnenus	1057–1059
Constantine X Ducas	1059–1067
Romanus IV Diogenes	1067–1071
Michael VII Ducas	1071–1078
Nicephorus III Botaniates	1078–1081
Alexius I Comnenus	1081–1118

CHAPTER ONE

When I woke up this morning, I could see through my window-slit that the winter sky was dark. I dressed in my rough robe and pushed open the door to the long, dim hallway. The stone floor was cold under my bare feet as I walked to the refectory door, where the sisters were lined up in their gray habits. We filed in, in silence, as usual, and sat down to a meal of porridge and milk.

I stared at the dreary food and listened to today's chosen sister droning a passage from the Bible. Suddenly my mind was flooded with the picture of the banquet my father had given on the occasion of my betrothal.

Once more, I sat on a high purple cushion in the great dining-hall of the palace. The bronze dishes gleamed in the bright torch-light; servers in multicolored uniforms poured great spouts of red wine into tall goblets; the rich smells of spices and roasted meats filled the room; the guests talked and laughed, teasing me and my betrothed, as was the custom; the dogs barked and fought over bones; my mother led the company in singing bridal songs that made me blush, child that I was.

The image was so strong that I forgot where I really was and did not realize how hard I gripped my wooden spoon until it broke in my clenched fist. I was confused for a moment to find myself sitting on the hard stone bench in the convent's refectory, with the reading sister hushed into silence, the others looking at me out of the corners of their eyes. The only face turned squarely in my direction was that of the mother superior.

"Are you troubled, my daughter?" she asked. "Is there something you lack?"

"Nothing, Mother," I murmured, and leaned forward to try to eat some of the porridge with what was left of my spoon. She said no more, but after the meal, she held me back.

"You have seemed dissatisfied of late. Can I do anything to make you more comfortable here?"

What could I say? That I was sick to death of the quiet, the dull grayness, the monotony of the days? There was nothing she, or I, could do to change that. I mentally searched the convent, looking for a glint of color, a place of warmth, and suddenly I remembered the scriptorium, the copying-room where the little nuns sat hunched over parchment, copying manuscripts in their careful handwriting. They were allowed a little more heat than the rest of the sisters, since frozen hands do not make graceful letters, and more light, so that they could see their work clearly. The talented were occasionally allowed a little pigment to adorn a capital letter, and occasionally even some gold leaf to decorate the first page of a manuscript.

"I would ask a favor," I replied finally. "My days are long and I do not have the duties that keep your women occupied. I am skilled at writing, and it would please me to spend a few hours every day assisting your sisters in the copying-room."

I had already learned that the mother had long trained her face not to show emotion, so I could not tell if she was surprised. She merely replied, "We would be grateful for your assistance and I would gladly grant you permission. But as you know, I must consult with the emperor before approving any change in your daily routine."

As she said this, I was glad that I was no less disciplined than she, for if my face had shown what I felt, I would have terrified the meek little women still lining the hallway with the sight of the bitter hatred that welled up in me at the mention of my brother. For it is his fault that I am here; his fault that my intelligence and my training are being wasted within these stone walls; his fault that I am not sitting on the high throne as empress of the

Byzantine Empire. For I am Anna Comnena, and I was born in the purple chamber, where the heirs to the throne of the most powerful empire in the world first see the light.

CHAPTER TWO

After the noon meal today, Mother Superior informed me that she had received word that "the emperor" had no objection to my copying manuscripts. He also sent me his prayers. Not that I want them.

So in the afternoon I left my room, and with a little nun as guide, made my way to the scriptorium. This convent is really just a large farmhouse, but it is old, and the wooden floors creak underfoot as you walk. My guide led me down the dark hall. The mother superior rarely allows either candles or torches, and the weak winter sun is not enough to illuminate these rooms.

Down the hall we went in silence, and then up the narrow stairs to the scriptorium, a small room on the corner of the building with window-slits facing west and south. What little sun there was shone through more brightly here, and a small fire burned in the hearth. I sat on a vacant stool. As no one paid me the least attention, I had leisure to look around.

Four nuns were perched on high wooden stools, bent over tables littered with paper, inks, pens, and short knives. Their sleeves were rolled up for greater ease in writing. Since they usually hide their hands in their wide sleeves, I was almost startled to see that they indeed had hands and wrists. I could not see their faces, and only occasionally would one shift position, heave a sigh, or rub her fingers, which must have been cramped from the work. A young novice in a white robe darted from one to the other, filling ink-pots, sharpening pens, cleaning brushes, all without saying a word. I wondered how she knew which sister needed attention.

For two hours I sat on a hard stool, hands folded on my lap, waiting for Sister Thekla, who is in charge of the scriptorium, to assign me a task. This sister walked up and down in front of the tables, occasionally pointing at something on a page without saying a word. The nun whose paper had been indicated would nod, then reach for the sharp knife kept handy to scrape off mistakes.

I had never spoken to Sister Thekla, but had ample opportunity to observe her as she walked up and down, pretending not to notice my existence. She is short and plain, with a mustache, and eyebrows that meet above her nose. She was evidently pleased to be able to make an imperial princess wait for her convenience. But I am patient. I know how to wait. I started learning patience before I was born.

As a child, I often heard my mother tell the story of my birth. Two days before I was born, in the year of Our Lord 1083, my mother, the Empress Irene Ducaena, felt me stirring in her belly and was worried that I would appear before my father came home from war. So she made the sign of the cross over me where I lay in her belly, and said, "Wait, Little One, until your father returns." Her mother told her she was being foolish, for what if my father were delayed for a month or more? Could she bear the pangs of labor that long? But fortunately for both of us, just two days later the emperor returned in triumph, and I was born in the great bedchamber hung with imperial purple, where all children of the emperor come into the world.

Now, I told myself, if I can wait two days to be born, out of respect for my mother's wishes, surely I can wait a few hours while a homely nun pretends to ignore me as I sit quietly on a stool.

I did not much mind the wait, in any case. It was good to smell the ink and hear the scratching of the pens once more. I have always loved learning, and as a child was the prize pupil of the imperial tutor and librarian, the eunuch Simon, a small man with no hair and a round belly. When he discovered my passion for the chronicles of our ancestors, he set me to memorizing large portions of the *Iliad*. "You can learn everything you need to know about life from this book, Little Beetle," he said to me. "It's all

7

there—love, hatred, life, death, immortality—everything you humans find important."

"*We* humans? But surely you are human, too, Simon?"

"Not really. Not anymore," he said. "A slave is not a human being, Princess; or were you not aware of that?"

I didn't like it when he talked like that. Father Agathos said that we should all be content to be where God had placed us. I had been born in the purple, and I was to marry the man my father had chosen as his heir, so I would be the next empress. Simon had been born the son of a schoolmaster in a village that had revolted against the rule of my father's family, the Comneni, so he and his family became slaves.

According to Father Agathos, this was logical, and a good instance of God's plan; for how could I be empress if there were no slaves? For me to fulfill my destiny, Simon had to fulfill his. I accepted this without question, as my mother had told me that Father Agathos was very wise. But it still made me uneasy.

My memories of Simon were interrupted by Sister Thekla, who suddenly appeared before me and glowered into my face. When I looked up at her, she turned on her heel and marched down to the end of one of the copy-desks. I assumed I was to follow, although at another time of my life, a common woman who turned her back on me would have been instantly banished from the empire. But I care for these forms no longer, and followed her to the place that had been recently vacated by one of the nun-scribes.

Sister Thekla nodded to the little novice, who scurried

8

up to my spot with a pen, a bottle of thin black ink, and a piece of parchment that had been used and reused so many times that the constant scraping had worn it almost away. Sister Thekla pointed to the top of the page and said, "*Alpha.*" She then turned on her heel and marched away once again.

I burned. She had set me the most elementary writing task, one that I had accomplished with skill and ease at the age of five. Yet if she wanted rows of the letter *alpha*, the first letter of the alphabet, *alpha* she would get.

As I clenched the pen, thinking how to begin, the novice appeared at my side. In front of me she placed a straight piece of wood and a pointed stick. These were for me to make straight lines across the paper, pressing the point of the stick into the paper to make a dent that would gradually disappear after I had written. As I reached for them, the girl gave me a shy smile, blinking at me with lashless eyes above a pink nose that ran. I did not return her smile. Did she not know who I was? Who was she to offer friendship to me? After all, I had learned what friendship meant, and did not trust it anymore.

For an hour I sat at my bench, making rows of *alpha*s. The first ones were simple, like those of a child, but I gradually embellished them, adorning them with curlicues and extravagant ornamentation. By the time I got to the bottom of the page, a reader could hardly tell what letter he was looking at, so hidden in the depth of the flourishes was the original *alpha*.

When I finally realized that I was cold and looked up, I saw that I was alone but for Sister Thekla, who was now seated at the end of the room. The other sisters had slipped out while I was working, and the small fire was reduced to embers and ashes. Not wishing to carry my work to the nun like a small child to her teacher, I folded my hands in my lap and stared straight ahead. Sister Thekla also sat with her hands in her lap, although she looked down at them and not at me. I could see her fingers moving over the beads of her rosary as her lips moved in prayer.

In silence we waited. I could tell that the sun was sinking ever lower, as the room grew darker and chillier. I was glad of my woolen cloak and wondered how the nun was standing the cold on her stone perch. Longer and longer we waited. I grew hungry and started to feel the need to visit the privy. Still we waited.

At last, I heard the convent bell begin to toll. I knew that Sister Thekla had to present herself at prayers, and that the mother superior was expecting to hear how I had performed at my task. Sister Thekla knew it too, and finally rose to her feet and came in my direction. She bent her head and looked at my writing. Without glancing at me or saying a word, she nodded, turned, and left the room.

I sat for another minute, so as not to follow Sister Thekla too closely, and then as I walked down the now-black corridor, I almost laughed out loud. I had triumphed, indeed, but what a triumph! A nun had tried to humiliate me even further than I had already been humiliated, and I had resisted. But what an enemy on whom to practice my long-studied arts of diplomacy and cunning.

I should have been dealing with a foreign prince, a bishop, a sultan, not with a little woman of no importance save in her own small world.

How had I fallen so far? Why were my feet not ringing on the polished marble floors of the palace in Constantinople? Why were servants not running to bring me delicate foods, to light a roaring fire in a tapestry-hung hall? Why were my feet covered with coarse shoes instead of silk slippers, and my hair gathered up in a loose knot instead of woven into complicated braids and lightly patted with perfume?

A small voice kept saying in time to my footsteps, "You did it yourself-yourself-yourself—you did it yourself-yourself-yourself," but I hushed it. If I had succeeded—if my mother and I had managed to accomplish what we had set out to do—if we had not been betrayed by those we most trusted—I would now be seated next to my husband in the imperial throne room, and that small, ugly man who calls himself the emperor and my brother would be buried in the cold, dark ground of Constantinople.

CHAPTER
THREE

There is no reason I should find it so hard to sleep; my bed is comfortable enough, and it is quiet. I hear the ringing of the bell summoning the nuns to prayer, and the rustle of their robes as they shuffle to the chapel. If I listen hard, I can hear their faint voices chanting downstairs, and then their footsteps as they return to their dormitories once more.

Some nights, as I lie here in the quiet, I look up at the low ceiling, then around at the bare stone walls, the narrow windows, the meager furnishings. My table is near the larger of the two windows, and when the moonlight is strong I can see the inkwell and scraps of paper that Sister Thekla has allowed me to take back to my room, to "practice my writing," she says. I did not tell her what is obvious to both of us: that my handwriting is clearer than that of any nun in the convent. As I left today she handed me a sheaf of old, torn paper, a worn-out pen, and some poor thin ink.

"Take these to your room," she instructed me. "While we sisters are praying, practice your letters."

Practice my letters, indeed! I have in mind a much better use for these materials. Since I cannot sleep, I will sit at my little table, and by the light of the moon, write down as many of my memories as come to me. I started with an account of my life here and my visit to the scriptorium, but these memories are nothing when compared with my life before I came to this barren place. It is these images that I wish to put on paper before they fade.

I am more recently arrived at the convent than are most of the sisters. Their recollections of their former days must be dim by now, and what they have to remember is probably of dreary lives on farms, or occasionally a small manor. My mind is filled with more glorious images.

Of course what I remember most is my family. My father used to joke that someday people would find it difficult to understand how we were all related to each other, especially after I married, because then our already complicated family trees would be intertwined. My betrothed, Constantine Ducas, came from royalty. His father had been Emperor Michael VII, and his stepfather Emperor Nicephorus III. His grandfather had also been emperor, and was also named Constantine, the tenth emperor of that name, and that Constantine's wife had been named Eudocia Dalassena.

The brother of Constantine X was the great-grandfather of my mother, Irene Ducas. As I worked it out, making ever more elaborate charts and lists, Constantine Ducas, my betrothed, was my third cousin. When he reached manhood and was crowned Constantine XI, he would marry me, his distant relation. Thus his right to rule would be assured, since he was not only a descendant of the old imperial line but would also be the son-in-law of the conquering emperor.

For we Comneni had conquered the Ducas emperors, thus restoring the throne to our family, which had already held it before the Ducases. My great-uncle Isaac Comnenus had briefly been emperor, only to be turned out of the palace by a Ducas. Isaac's sister-in-law, my grandmother Anna Dalassena, had burned (so she later told me, over and over again) at the insult, and when her favorite son, my father, Alexius, grew to manhood, she helped him regain the throne that had rightfully belonged to us. Ever after she hated the Ducases.

But this had all happened before I was born. As far as I knew, we had always lived in the palace. My beautiful, gentle mother had always been empress, and my powerful father had always been emperor.

My earliest memory is of a day when I was only five years old. Simon had dismissed the students and was following us out of the classroom. I caught sight of myself in one of the polished corridor mirrors. I was wearing a new robe of bright green silk, and I turned slowly, admiring myself. Simon, seeing me, said, "What are you doing, Princess?"

"Just looking," I answered, continuing to turn. The color made my eyes look like emeralds, I thought. "I am more beautiful than Aphrodite!" I exclaimed, then stopped short as Simon clapped his hand over my mouth.

"Hush!" he said. "Don't ever say such a thing! Don't you know what happens to those who try to outshine the gods? Don't you remember Niobe, who bragged that she had more children than Leto, the mother of Apollo and Artemis?"

"Yes," I said, proud to show off how attentively I had listened to his lessons. "Apollo and Artemis came down and shot her children with arrows to punish their mother's pride."

"That's right," he said. "Do you want the same to happen to you?"

"That's nonsense," I told him. "Father Agathos says that when Christ was born all the old gods died."

"That may be, and it may not," he said. "But it doesn't pay to take chances." I knew my mother disapproved of such heathen talk, but Simon spoke with the authority of one who knew about such things. I wondered if he knew something my mother and Father Agathos didn't.

My cousins had by now disappeared outside, and I ran after them. The nurse caught me as I tried to slip out to the playing field.

"Where have you been?" she demanded, and not waiting for my answer, started pulling me out of the women's quarters. "We have been looking for you. There is a delegation of foreign ambassadors here to meet the emperor's family."

Normally I would have objected to the idea of an audience with old men who did not even speak Greek, but this day I was pleased to show off my new dress. They would praise my beauty, my royal bearing, my intelligence, as they always did. I was too young to know that this was mere courtier's flattery, meant to please my father, so I followed my nurse to the throne room without protest.

I arrived at the great hall and peeked in the door. Under the high dome, glittering with mosaics, my parents sat on their thrones, my modest mother with a hood drawn over her face, as always when strange men were present. I had not seen her in several days, and if it had not been for the formal-looking crowd nearby, I would have run to her embrace. As it was, I walked slowly and precisely, as I had been taught, through the dark room. I kept my hands folded in front of me and my eyes fixed on the floor. I watched my feet in their green slippers pass over different-colored blocks of marble: gray with white flecks, green serpentine, rich black, and the blood-red porphyry that only the emperor's family was allowed to use. When I saw the feet of my father's throne, I moved into my position at his right hand, between the two tall thrones covered with gold leaf and smelling faintly of the cedar wood of which they were made. Only then did I look up.

My father sat upright. As always, he was at his best when seated; you could not see that he was short, and his dark hair and beard looked especially impressive with the gold and bright jewels of his crown. He glanced down at me and frowned, but since the foreign ambassadors were already there, and indeed appeared to be concluding their business, he did not chide me for my tardiness. I moved closer to my mother's side, where I saw our nurse holding my sister, Maria, who was then two years old. Behind my father, as always, stood his mother, my grandmother Anna Dalassena. Above the veil covering her mouth and chin, her large dark eyes slanted up toward her temples. She did not say anything, but her eyes flickered sideways in my direction. Her right hand rested lightly on the back of my father's throne, and he seemed to lean slightly into it as he sat.

My father stood to indicate that the formal part of the audience was over. He and the ambassadors were smiling, so I assumed all had gone well with their business, which meant that my father would be in a good mood that evening.

"Tell our guests that I wish to present the imperial children to them," my father said, turning to the interpreter. "This is my firstborn, the Princess Anna Porphyrogenita." He smiled a secret smile at me, and instantly I felt better. He might act stern in front of visitors, but I knew my father loved me more than he loved anyone else.

I stepped forward and bowed to the ambassadors, then stepped back.

"My second-born, Princess Maria Porphyrogenita," he went on, and Maria's nurse moved forward one step and bowed, while Maria bent her head with its cap of red-gold hair.

"Lastly, my youngest child, Prince John Porphyrogenitus."

John? Who was John Porphyrogenitus? Then I saw the cradle next to my mother's throne. Had we had a baby? Is that where my mother had been? Forgetting that I was not to move until the barbarians had left, I drew nearer to the cradle but could not see inside for the crowd of men bending over it. They finally withdrew and one of them spoke to the interpreter, who addressed my father:

"Your Majesty must be warmly congratulated on the birth of so lovely a son, the heir to your throne."

The room spun around me. What were they talking about? I was my father's firstborn, and my betrothed, Constantine Ducas, was to inherit the throne. I had known this all my life. I felt a wail of protest rising up in me, but I caught my grandmother's glittering eye fixed on me with such ferocity that I fought it down fiercely.

But I need not have worried; my father was speaking. "Tell the ministers that they are mistaken. The heir is my daughter, Anna. She is betrothed to my wife's young cousin, Constantine Ducas. When they wed, they will unite the Ducas and Comnenus families, ending any dispute over which family has the right to rule."

The ambassadors reacted to this news by turning to each other and babbling in their strange tongue (Venetian, I later found out). The interpreter listened, then turned to my father.

"I beg Your Majesty's pardon," he said, "but they have never before heard of the custom of a woman inheriting when there is a son. Nor have they heard of the ruler choosing his heir. In their part of the world, either the people elect the ruler, or the oldest son of the king becomes heir—"

"Leading to the degeneracy of their countries," interrupted my grandmother. "Even if the firstborn son is an idiot or a criminal, he must inherit. No wonder the petty lordlings of the West are continually arguing with each other, unable to agree among themselves."

"Do not translate that," my father said hastily to his interpreter. "Merely tell them that it is our custom that the emperor choose the one he feels most suited to rule after him, man or woman, relative or no."

The interpreter spoke. The ambassadors smiled, nodding. But their eyes looked puzzled.

The business seemed to be over, so I waited for the ambassadors to turn their attention to me, as they always did. I knew that they had never seen such a beautiful green dress, and that they would exclaim over my royal bearing, my gravity beyond my years, and my strong resemblance to my father. But instead they merely thanked my father for their audience, and finally bowed themselves out, without glancing at me or Maria, or even paying their respects to our mother. One of them did shoot a curious look at my grandmother as she stood rock-still behind the throne.

My family, which I supposed must now include the cradle and its occupant, was left alone. I drew near the cradle and finally was able to see into it.

Had a monkey escaped from my father's zoo? I saw a tiny, wrinkled face; black fur over most of the head and face; little, beady eyes; yellow skin. This was the beauty they were all exclaiming over? My grandmother's words returned to me: "if the firstborn son is an idiot or a criminal." Which one was this baby? And if he was one or the other, why were we keeping him?

"Mother——" I started to say, but she was already rising from her throne. She had let the hood fall back from her head, showing her face and her red-gold hair. She looked thinner than I remembered, and she was pale.

"Anna, I must get some rest. I should not even have been out of bed today, but this audience was important. I will speak to you tomorrow."

"But, Mother——" I started again. And again she silenced me with a look, and followed by the nurse carrying Maria, and a new nurse carrying the baby, she walked out the door with my father. My grandmother followed.

Later, the afternoon turned hot and the buzzing of the flies was even louder than the chatter of the servants. Everyone had retired to their bedchambers to sleep away the hottest part of the day. I lay in my bed, remembering the events of the audience. It was unfair. I was always the one visitors paid attention to. No one had ever wondered over my right to the throne, as these barbarians had. Could they have planted a seed of doubt in my father's mind? He was always telling us that we had to be kind to our enemies—would that include making them like him more if he followed their ways?

And my mother's refusal to stay with me, after I had not seen her for so long, burned me. I knew that women who had just had babies were tired. My aunts usually did not even leave their rooms for weeks after childbirth. It was all that stupid baby's fault, I thought, as I buried my face in my hot pillow, willing myself not to sleep, to stay awake and figure out how to win my mother back to me. If there were no baby, she would be here now, turning my pillow over to the cool side, ordering a slave to fan me, stroking my hair until I fell asleep. She would be singing to Maria, who still needed a lullaby. But instead, she was with *him*. I suddenly realized that even if she couldn't come to me, I could go to her. I could convince her that we were much happier before the baby had been born, that Maria and I were surely enough for her.

Maria's nurse was occupied in trying to get her to sleep, in the bed she was sharing with me. Now I understood why she was not in her cradle anymore. Since no one was paying much attention to what I did, I slipped out of our bedroom and ran down the hall to my mother's room. To my disappointment, I saw she was asleep, her face looking worn, and older than I remembered. Maria's old cradle was next to her bed, with the drowsy new nurse nodding on a stool nearby. The nurse roused herself and looked up at the sound of my footsteps, and held her finger to her lips. I nodded, to show I understood.

I crept up to the cradle. The baby was asleep, his furry head black against the pillow. We don't need him, I thought. If he were gone, everything would be the way it was before. The ambassadors would not ignore me, and they would never again think someone else was my father's heir. Mother wouldn't be so tired, and she would be spending her time with me and Maria, instead of with this ugly little thing.

I had a thought that made my heart beat with excitement.

"Look how beautiful he is," I said in as loud a tone as I dared. I looked up to see if any heavenly arrows were falling. Nothing. The nurse smiled, nodding her approval that I was admiring the baby.

"He is as beautiful as a little god," I declared in a louder voice. "More beautiful even than Apollo." I looked out the window. Still nothing but serene blue sky.

Simon was wrong. There were no gods anymore to punish injustice. I would have to do it myself.

CHAPTER FOUR

It is not strange for me to live here now, in this community of women. Unlike some of the degenerate western countries of which I have read, and whose representatives I met during the Crusade, the women of Byzantium do not mix with men. We have our own palaces, or at least our own apartments in a larger palace. The little boys stay with the women until they reach the age when they need training in arms, and then they move to the men's quarters.

My mother fell ill shortly after John was born, and passed on much of his care to the nurse, who happily took complete charge of him. She kept him somewhat apart from the rest of us, to give my mother a rest.

And when my mother recovered, John was more used to his nurse and was so spoiled that my mother's strictness provoked screams and tantrums from him. So the nurse took over his care even more than she had for Maria and me.

This situation was entirely to my liking; I was used to babies and usually enjoyed playing with them, but this little boy irritated me. He was a whiny child, who screamed for what he wanted until the indulgent nurse gave in. His sharp eyes never missed anything, and we soon learned to hide toys and sweets away when he was present, for we would be forced to hand them over to him if he caught sight of them.

So I was more familiar with my sister and cousins than with my brother. There were many cousins, some close to my age, and we played ball, ran races, and had make-believe games of Byzantine knights conquering hordes of infidel Turks. When it was cold or rainy, we stayed indoors, playing dice and hiding from each other in the palace's many rooms. We also had lessons together. I had started studying with Simon when I was four years old, learning the rudiments of reading, mathematics, logic, and other studies suitable for imperial children. Simon set us difficult lessons, but he was a kind master, and those of us who applied ourselves received our share of praise.

I enjoyed all these pursuits, especially my letters, but was not pleased on those occasions when my father's mother, Anna Dalassena, appeared in the schoolroom to inspect us. Since we were all children except for the harmless Simon, she would come with her face unveiled. Her long lips always curved into a satisfied smile when we stood up from our benches and bowed deeply to her. She asked us many questions, and her manner was so severe that the answers to even the easiest questions would flee our minds under her interrogation. Even worse than a wrong answer was none at all, and I heard my cousins in their desperation give ridiculous answers, such as "seven," when asked how many popes there had been up to the present, or "air, fire, water, and wine" when queried as to the four elements, rather than show their ignorance.

One day, two years after I had first met my brother, we older imperial children were engrossed in the study of astronomy when our grandmother appeared. We had our backs to the door and knew of her arrival only when Simon stopped speaking in midsentence and prostrated himself on the floor. We all knew what that meant, and without looking around, leaped to our feet and bowed our heads as low as we could.

Grandmother walked slowly into the room, her long robes swishing and her shoes clicking on the hard floor. We all stood still, scarcely daring to breathe. As she passed me, I glanced up under my eyelashes, expecting to see her back as she continued her inspection. Instead, I found that she had turned and was looking at me. My face burned when I realized that she had caught me acting less than respectful, and I was thankful that I had not inherited my mother's pearly skin, as Maria had. Perhaps in the shadows she could not see how red I was turning. But I knew that punishment was sure to follow. I was the oldest, and was expected to set a good example for the younger children. And my grandmother often seemed to turn her wrath on me more than on the others. What would it be this time? A caning? Fasting on bread and water? Please, I prayed inwardly, do not make me kneel on the stone floor of the chapel during the afternoon rest. My knees ached as I remembered the cold roughness pressing into my bare skin just the month before, when I had been punished for not knowing the names of my paternal ancestors for seven generations back.

"Why do you look at me?" she demanded, her voice even.

I knew that my grandmother admired boldness and that hesitation was a sin in her eyes, so I answered promptly, even though I hardly knew what I was saying.

"I was hoping you had passed me and would find someone else to criticize," I said.

She let out a snort that might have been laughter, except that her face did not change into a smile, as my father's would have done.

"Do you think I criticize too much?" she asked.

"Yes," I answered. "You let pass faults in others that you punish in me."

"And why do you think that is?" she persisted.

Although I knew it would be better to answer immediately, I was afraid to tell the truth.

"Tell me," she said.

Reluctantly, I spoke. "I think you don't like me very much."

Silence. My eyes were fixed on the floor once more, and this time I did not dare to look up. The silence grew longer and more uncomfortable. I heard my sister and cousins shift their weight as they grew tired of standing still. I wondered where Simon was, and if, like the rest of us, he had his face turned downward, or if he had the courage to watch what was happening. I resigned myself to at least a few hours on my knees, and perhaps no real food for a few days.

Finally, I could bear it no longer. I raised first my eyes, then my chin, and found that my grandmother was looking me full in the face. Her expression was hard to read—was it pity? Sorrow? And mixed with what—triumph? Joy?

"There you are wrong," she said, with an unexpected gentleness that startled me. "I treat you with more strictness because more is expected of you. Come." She strode back out the door she had entered, forcing me to sidle out from my bench and break into a trot as I went. I glanced back at Simon, knowing that I was breaking his cardinal rule of not cleaning my work space before leaving, but what could I do? And in any case, I feared my grandmother many times more than I feared the little tutor.

As I entered the corridor, I could see the end of my grandmother's long gown as she swung around a corner. I ran, hoping no one would see me behaving in such an unseemly manner indoors. Where could she be going?

I received my answer as I turned the next corner and saw her waiting for me, at the entrance to the throne room. Her hand was on the hanging, holding it open. The guards on either side of the door were standing stiffly erect, although I was sure they must be wondering what was going on. "Come in," she said impatiently, as though she had been waiting for hours instead of seconds.

I passed through the hanging and entered the vast hall. The throne room was dark, since the torches were lighted only when the emperor was present. The light that shone in the windows made strange patterns on the multicolored floor. It all looked dead, somehow, without my parents and the attendants that accompanied them wherever they went.

The two thrones stood side by side on a low platform, my father's with its ornate carving and rich gold ornamentation, and my mother's, more simple, but no less beautiful. They looked strange and oddly shaped when empty. Aside from my parents' seats at the banquet table, these were the only chairs with backs and arms I had ever seen.

"Come closer," my grandmother said. Hardly daring to breathe, I took a step forward, then another, expecting at any moment to see my father burst in and demand to know what I was doing there. I almost hoped he would; his anger was easy to bear, and it would free me from whatever it was my grandmother was planning. With an impatient sound, my grandmother reached out a hand and pulled me up the step to the thrones themselves.

"There," she said. "There you see what awaits you."

Puzzled, I looked more closely at the thrones. The sweet smell of cedar reached my nostrils and made me sneeze. Even in the dimness, the gold glinted, and the ornate carving cast complicated shadows. But I could not see what she meant about what awaited me. There were no words carved into the wood, and the designs were abstract geometric shapes, not scenes of any future life.

"Sit down," commanded my grandmother.

How could I? I was sure that if I so much as touched the wood an earthquake would shake me to the depths of the earth, or lightning would strike through the window and sizzle me where I stood, or a giant eagle would seize me in its talons and bear me to Hell. But as I hesitated, I saw her brows draw together and her face begin to scowl. Eager to do anything to avoid her anger, I walked to my mother's throne and moved to sit in it.

"Not there!" she snapped. "That throne is for the follower! It is for the Ducas!" She spat the last word with such venom that I shrank back, terrified. She must have seen how afraid I was, for she softened somewhat, and said in a milder tone, indicating the larger of the thrones, "You must sit here. You must sit where a Comnenus sits, see what a Comnenus sees, think what a Comnenus thinks."

My heart raced as I approached the imperial throne. I hesitated, swallowed, then said to myself what I imagined Simon would say to me if he were there, "Come, it is but a chair, and you have sat in many chairs." I stood on the footstool, grasped the throne's arms, covered in purple velvet, and pulled myself up, then sat and looked out over the throne room. The seat cushion that discreetly raised my father to nearly my mother's height was missing, and the hard wood felt cold on my body. I gripped the armrests to keep from slipping to the back.

Why did it all look different? I had been there hundreds of times, usually mere inches away from where I was sitting. But something had changed. Everything was now below me, including the tall figure, robed in black, that was Anna Dalassena.

"See," she said, "see how it will appear to you," and she walked back to the door, then made a pretense of entering, walking with the small, hesitant steps of a frightened suppliant. I stifled a laugh, but she must have heard, for she looked up quickly and smiled at me as though in complicity. Her footsteps rang hollowly in the empty room as she approached the throne, then bowed low, as a courtier does to his lord.

After a moment she raised herself up again. "See how they will bow to you, how they will worship you, how they will fear you. A word from you can bring death, or can bring an end to war. Your enemies will tremble, and your friends will tremble too, because they know how quickly the empress's friendship can turn to enmity."

Her voice was lulling me into a trance. I saw myself, looking like my father but for the beard, short and dark, yes, but who saw that when you sat on the imperial throne? I saw the heavy crown glitter on my head, the purple slippers on my feet being kissed by kings and princes. I saw my word starting wars and ending them. I saw great churches rise where I so commanded, and ships depart from port on my order.

She stopped talking, and with the silence I woke from my reverie. I sat, a seven-year-old girl, on a throne that was so big for me that my feet did not even reach the purple cushion placed in front of it to disguise how short my father's legs were. How could I ever learn what to do? The hugeness of the task terrified me.

"But, Grandmother," I said, my voice croaking. I cleared my throat and started again. "But, Grandmother, I don't know how to do all those things."

She came closer and bent down to me, her nose nearly meeting mine. I willed myself to hold still, to return her gaze without flinching. Suddenly she smiled, not a joyous smile, but one I could surely read as triumphant this time.

"But I do," she said.

CHAPTER FIVE

And so my real education began. My grandmother had a little room set up for us near the schoolroom, and several times each week she would interrupt my lessons with Simon and take me there. I would rise from my books, feeling the eyes of the others on me, and conscious of my own superiority, would follow my grandmother into our study. I always left my books and papers in disarray, knowing that my grandmother would not permit me to delay long enough to clean them up, and also knowing that no one would dare complain about the extra work of clearing my space.

My grandmother never referred to books in her tutoring. Rather, she spoke rapidly, telling me about the different countries surrounding our empire, about their rulers, about who was related to whom, about what languages they spoke. She told me about battles, about weapons, about warriors—she had been on so many campaigns with my grandfather and his brother that she knew almost as much about warcraft as any soldier did. My head reeled as I tried to take it all in, frantically scribbling notes that I would consult later in the classroom after the other children had been dismissed to play. It was difficult, but I was proud that it was I, not John, who was learning all this. No one would ever think he was the heir again!

My training did not stop there. When I was ten, my grandmother convinced my father to allow me to gain some practical knowledge at his side. I learned how difficult it was to govern an empire as vast as ours. My father rose before dawn every morning and started seeing ambassadors, kings, courtiers, and petitioners before the rest of the family had even had breakfast. On the days when he permitted me to attend, I stood behind a screen on my father's left, so that the eyes of men would not fall on me. When the light was right, I could see through the screen's fine fabric. I got to know all my father's advisors by sight, mostly gray-headed old men in long robes who didn't look very interesting. But my eyes were always drawn to a tall young man with golden hair who stood close to my father on his right hand. The youth dressed like an athlete in a short tunic and high boots, and he carried himself with grace.

One day, in the summer when I turned eleven, I had spent the hot afternoon indoors. My father had had no pressing affairs of state, so I had not attended the audiences in the throne room. John had as usual not come to the schoolroom, and my cousins had finished their work the day before while I had been learning statecraft, so I was alone with Simon. He had finally relented when I told him how my head ached over the geometry problems he had set me, and said I might rest while we talked.

"It's so hot," I complained. "Why does the sun have to be so close? If it were farther away we would be cooler."

"It's close indeed," Simon said, "as Icarus found out. Do you remember that story?"

"Well enough," I answered. It was not my favorite story, but anything was better than geometry. "Icarus and his father Daedalus were imprisoned in a tower—I forget why—and his father made them wings out of feathers and wax. They flew away from their prison. Daedalus told Icarus not to fly too high, but he disobeyed, and the sun melted the wax, and his wings came apart. He fell into the ocean and drowned."

Simon nodded. He looked thoughtful, although I could see little in the story to think about. Icarus had been a foolish and disobedient boy, and had been punished—what was there to say?

"May I go outside now?" I asked. I could hear someone playing in the courtyard and burned to join in.

"In a moment, Little Beetle." Simon was still looking thoughtful. I hoped he wasn't going to turn that simple story into a lesson. But of course he did.

"Why do you think Icarus had to die?" he asked me.

"He disobeyed his father," I answered.

"But his father wasn't the emperor, merely a common man," he said. "Wouldn't death be a harsh punishment for so small a crime?" I shrugged, not really interested.

Simon kept on. "What is the sun?" he asked.

This was getting even more tedious. "Heat..." I hazarded, but Simon frowned and shook his head, so I went on. "Light, the source of life, power..." I kept talking, hoping to hit the right answer. I must have found it with my last guess, for he nodded.

"Exactly. The father saw his son approaching manhood and was jealous of having to share his power. He tried to keep the boy a child too long. Icarus tried to become a man before he was ready, making up his own mind about things better left to his elders. *That* was his crime, and death was his punishment."

I nodded impatiently, trying to see out the window. Simon seemed about to speak again, but instead he sighed and dismissed me. My sister, Maria, was waiting for me faithfully, as she always did, and together with our cousins we ran out to the polo ground.

We had crossed the compound and entered the field when suddenly a huge brown horse came galloping toward us, so close that I could feel the hoofbeats in my chest. The other children scattered, but I froze. Just as I was sure I was about to be trampled, I felt myself being swooped up and realized I was seated with my father on his great black charger. He held me so tightly that the heavy gold ring on his right hand bruised my upper arm. But I didn't mind; he had not been holding me on his lap of late and I had missed it. I sat rigidly, wishing I could melt into him the way Maria did. But my long legs hung down the side of the horse, reminding me that I was not a little girl anymore. I looked up at my father, hoping to see his rare smile, but found that he was looking not at me, but at the disappearing brown horse.

"Constantine!" he shouted. The rider of the brown horse glanced back over his shoulder, then turned his horse in our direction. He slowed to a trot and approached. I saw a handsome young blond man, with a straight back, and freckles. He carried himself with a grace and ease that were familiar. I was puzzled; who was he? I liked his smile, and the way he managed his horse. But there were many Constantines in our palace, and I had no idea which one this man—a boy, really, I saw as he drew nearer—was. Then I realized where I had seen him before.

"Do you know me, Princess?" the young man asked as he approached. I looked up at my father, and he nodded, giving me permission to speak.

"I think you are my mother's cousin who stands next to my father in the throne room," I answered.

The young man glanced at my father.

"An observant one," he said. "I didn't know if she would recognize me out of court." Then to me, "Yes, Princess, I am your cousin Constantine Ducas. I am pleased you recognized me."

My father gave a little snort of laughter. "Next time, be more careful when you race over the field where the children are playing," he said to Constantine, but I could tell he was more amused than angry. "You don't want to trample your future bride in the dust!" He gave me a kiss, then swung me down off the saddle. I stood in the middle of the field, all alone, ignoring the shouts of my cousins who were calling me to join them.

Future bride? The thought made me stand still. So this was the man I was to marry. I knew that my father had decided that one of my mother's cousins was to be my husband. It had something to do with the problem of my father's right to the throne; some people thought that a Ducas should be in power instead. But it had never occurred to me that the blond young man was my betrothed. I considered my father's choice, looking after him as he disappeared around a building. Constantine looked like the ideal husband: Evidently he liked to play games, and he was a good horseman. He was also very handsome. I suddenly pictured him on my father's cedar throne, myself on my mother's throne next to him. Would he smile at me when he thought no one was looking, the way my father did to my mother? Would he speak to me in a low voice, his face next to mine under our heavy crowns?

I did not know many young men. I knew that my father had chosen Constantine Ducas for my husband, so he had to be a worthy person. But I knew many worthy people. Would I want to be married to them? My husband had to be a good ruler, an honorable person, and a strong soldier to protect our empire. But I knew I wanted more than that. The young man's smile stayed with me as I stood still in thought, in the middle of the field.

My cousins and Maria were calling me. But I ignored

them. After all, I would be married within two or three years, to a soldier and a counselor of the emperor. I decided that my days of racing and playing tag were over. I walked slowly back to the compound, suddenly conscious of my bare legs, my loose hair, and the lack of a veil to cover my face. I felt naked, where ten minutes before I had been perfectly comfortable. I needed to seek out my mother and get properly dressed.

As I stepped through the arched doorway, I thought I had made a mistake and entered the wrong building. Instead of the usual calm, all was confusion. People were bustling around, giving orders, obeying orders, carrying bundles, opening trunks and moving their contents to boxes. I stood with my back to the wall, watching and listening. People were talking, and it was hard to understand any one voice among the many. But soon one word fell on my ears: "War!"

This was news indeed, but not unexpected. The Seljuk Turks had been attacking the empire with ever-increasing boldness, and the emperor had asked the pope for troops to help subdue them. The pope must have agreed, and my father must be getting ready once more to set off for battle. Within a few hours they were gone—my father, Constantine, and hundreds of soldiers. The palace seemed empty without them, but we were used to the emperor's frequent absences. He always came back weary, travel-stained, sometimes with a battle wound, but glorious in victory, and bearing presents.

But what of Constantine? He did not look old enough to have been in any battles yet. Would he know what to do? Would he be able to defend himself, and acquit himself honorably? I knew that my father, despite being emperor, still rode in the first ranks of the soldiers, fighting as hard and as bravely as anyone else. Would he protect Constantine, an unproven soldier? I shuddered as I remembered that my father had been only fourteen when he had fought in his first battle, and Constantine looked older than that.

I needed to do something to help him. When we were married, I could go along on the campaigns with him, and see to his wounds, and make sure that he was comfortable between battles. But now, I was helpless. The best I could do was to pray to St. Irene, my mother's patroness and the saint of peace, to stay by him, and to make the war end soon.

I was not to have much time to worry, however. Diplomatic duties did not end with my father's absence. Instead, I was required to attend even more of them. My father's mother, Anna Dalassena, commanded my presence whenever dignitaries were in attendance. My father owed his throne, at least in part, to her intelligence, and he trusted her more than anyone else. My mother never showed any interest in statecraft, so it was to Anna Dalassena that the emperor turned when in need of counsel.

The war lasted far longer and was more complicated than anyone had thought, and was grandly called a Crusade, or war for the Holy Cross. This Crusade would turn out to be just the first of several, although we did not know that at the time. Foreign soldiers, rulers, ambassadors, and traders of all sorts flooded the city as they prepared to join my father's troops, and we were forced to deal with them.

My grandmother sat in my father's high throne, wearing imperial robes. The differences between them became even more obvious when I saw her in my father's accustomed place. She was tall where he was short, and she had large, slanted eyes, where his were round and open. His hair was short, and simply dressed, as befitted a soldier, whereas her long black hair was arranged in the most complicated coils and braids I had ever seen. I would spend long minutes during these audiences trying to trace one strand of hair as it wound through a braid, across her head, down a tress, behind her ear. I would always lose the strand and have to start over. This practice would make me so sleepy that I would have to stop and pay attention to the speeches in an attempt to keep awake.

One day the baron of some small province had come to ask my grandmother for a reduction in taxes. As I listened to his pleas, and to my grandmother's skillful way of rejecting them, I began to see the encounter as a kind of game. A new game called chess was wildly popular in the palace. The rules were not very complicated, but there were endless strategies for dealing the death blow to the opponent's king. I pictured the baron, dressed in his shabby best, as a weak little pawn on a chessboard as he pled his pitiful case.

"Your Majesty," he said, facedown on the floor, "the crops have been poor after a long drought in our province. My people have been starving. Most of the men have left for the war, and there are few to work the fields. The foreigners have brought illness with them, and many of my people have died. What little they have managed to grow, they have eaten, with nothing left over to pay taxes."

"This is not the emperor's concern," responded my grandmother. "Your farmers must have committed some sin for God to punish them by withholding the rain." Aha, I thought—her bishop has attacked the pawn.

"Indeed not," protested the baron, daring to look up. "We are a God-fearing folk."

"Then why do you ask me to reduce your taxes at a time when the emperor needs all the funds he can raise to win the Holy City of Jerusalem back from the infidels?" she questioned him. Now her knight was on the attack. The baron was silent. I wondered if, like me, he could see chess pieces, one by one, being swept off the board.

"And besides," added my grandmother, "I have no power to reduce the taxes. This is in the emperor's hands, and I would be stealing from him if I allowed you to pay less than your requirement."

Shah mat, I thought. Checkmate. The king is dead. The baron probably knew as well as I did that whenever my father left the country, he signed a proclamation giving my grandmother imperial powers. But the baron did not dare contradict her to her face, so he left defeated.

After this I started looking forward to the audiences, to see what weapons my grandmother would pull out. Sometimes she was a chess player, and other times she reminded me of a fencer, probing the enemy's weak spots until she could lunge in with the kill. But no matter what tactic she took, she always won.

Once, as I was leaving the audience room, she unexpectedly called me over to her. I approached in a seemly manner and knelt at her feet. She pulled me up, putting her hand under my chin and forcing me to look at her. She stared into my eyes with her dark strange ones until I squirmed inside. But I did not look away.

"What do you think of all this?" she asked, waving her hand at the huge room, the thrones, the tapestries, the glittering mosaics on the walls and ceiling.

I shook my head, not knowing what to say.

"Come, child," she said impatiently, her bony hand still clutching my chin. "Surely you have some opinion."

I opened my mouth, not knowing what I was going to say until the words spilled out. "I think it's *wonderful*," I answered.

She barked a short laugh. "Wonderful, is it?" She finally let go of my chin. "And what is it you find so wonderful?"

"The throne—the p-p-power—" I stammered. "When I am empress, I will be able to deal with people the way I want to. I won't have to listen to anyone."

"Anyone? Will not your husband have something to say about it?"

I shrugged, feeling myself relax as she seemed interested in what I had to say. "Constantine will be emperor only because he is married to me. If he disagrees with me, I will still be able to have my way."

"And other counselors?"

I considered the question seriously before answering. "I

suppose I'll listen to their advice and then make up my own mind."

She stared into my eyes still, tapping her hand lightly on her knee. Finally, "Leave, child; go back to your studies," she said, and turned away.

I bowed again, rose, and walked away, managing to keep from running until I was out of the room. Once out of her sight, I tore to the library, where I found Simon at his books, and breathlessly related the conversation.

"What do you think she meant?" I asked.

He looked away from me and was silent for so long that I thought he hadn't heard me. At last, "Don't fly too near to the sun, Little Beetle," he said.

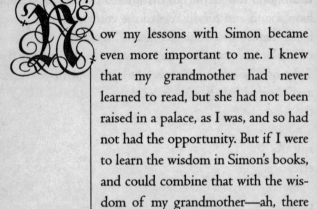ow my lessons with Simon became even more important to me. I knew that my grandmother had never learned to read, but she had not been raised in a palace, as I was, and so had not had the opportunity. But if I were to learn the wisdom in Simon's books, and could combine that with the wisdom of my grandmother—ah, there would never be a wiser ruler!

John, by contrast, rarely made an appearance in the classroom. But one day, Maria and I were hard at our geometry when we heard a commotion outside the classroom door. It was John's voice, and as usual, he was crying and protesting. My sister and I exchanged glances, and though we kept our heads down as though concentrating on our circles and triangles, we got no work done, but waited to see what was happening.

The door burst open, and a guard came in, leading John by the hand. Close behind them was our mother, her mouth set grimly. John was digging his nails into the guard's huge wrist in an attempt to free himself, but the guard ignored the scratches as though he did not even feel them. John shouted up to his expressionless face, "I will have you put to death! I will have you blinded and your hands cut off and your tongue cut out and your head cut off!" The guard stood impassively as Simon watched the scene quietly, his hands tucked in his long sleeves. Maria and I had given up all pretense of working and stared at the red-faced little boy.

Our mother moved in front of John, who was trying to spit in the guard's face. He was so small, though, that his efforts fell far short of their goal.

"John!" she said firmly. He ignored her. "John!" she repeated. "You must be quiet! The empress commands it!"

"But—" he wailed.

"Silence!" She glared at him, and he finally fell silent, trembling with rage, tears staining his cheeks.

My mother waited a moment, then went on in a gentler voice. "Simon tells me," she said, "that you have not been in this classroom for weeks. Don't you know that it is the wish of your father, the *emperor*"—she emphasized this last word—"that you learn to read?" John turned his head away but did not say a word. Our mother sighed, then motioned to Simon. "Bring him a book," she said, "the book that Anna first learned to read." Simon turned and rummaged in a box, pulled out a little psalm-book, and placed it, open, on the desk in front of the boy.

"Read it, child," went on my mother in a gentle voice. John stared down at the page, but did not say a word. My mother turned to Simon.

"You are the imperial tutor," she said, "and have taught all the children to read. Tell me, why has John not learned?"

"I do not know," said Simon. "The boy is not unintelligent." He shot an apprehensive glance at John, as though worried that the boy might start screaming again at this weak praise. But John made no reaction. Simon moved in front of John and pointed to the page. "What letter is this?" he asked. "*Zeta*," said John sullenly. "And this?" Simon pointed out several letters in a row, and each time John identified it correctly. "And the word it spells is . . . ?" asked Simon.

John stared down at the page and his face grew more and more red. Suddenly he stood up, threw the book across the room, and shouted, "I don't know! I don't know! And why do I need to read anyway? I'm going to be a soldier, and I will have scribes to read to me! Reading is not for soldiers! It is for women and slaves!" And with that he ran from the room, with the guard in hot pursuit.

My mother stayed where she was. She seemed to have forgotten that the rest of us were there. "Simon," she said, "I do not understand."

"Nor I," said Simon ruefully, rubbing his bald head as he did when worried. "There were some children who were pupils of my father's." He paused, and I sat still, hoping he would forget my presence and go on. Simon rarely mentioned his boyhood, at least in front of us children, and it was mysterious and exotic to me. He went on, "Not frequently, but once every few years, my father would tell my mother about his great frustration in not being able to teach some children how to read. Dunces he could understand and even teach, after a fashion, but some of the others baffled him. He said it was as though they had a blind area in their minds."

"And how did he finally teach them?" my mother asked.

Simon shook his head. "He didn't, Your Majesty," he said. "He would refund the school fees to their parents and send them home." My mother shook her head, looking out the door through which John had run. And without a word to the rest of us, she too left.

I never saw John in the classroom again. Maria later told me that he never returned, but as time went on I spent more and more of my day with my grandmother and probably would not have seen him anyway.

My grandmother was an excellent storyteller. I would sometimes sit with my hand idle, forgetting to take notes, while she told me of campaigns she had gone on with her husband, my grandfather. My mother had also accompanied my father to several battles, but unlike my grandmother, she did not like to tell of what she had seen in war. She said that war was a necessary evil, and that the sooner humans learned to do without it, the better.

My grandmother was evidently not of that opinion. Her descriptions of complicated battle-engines, of glorious charges, of strange foreigners who used different weapons that we could adapt to our own purposes made her eyes glitter with joy as she remembered them.

But we also had less exciting pursuits to study. Diplomacy, she assured me again and again, was even more effective than war. I had to learn, she informed me, to get what I wanted out of people in such a way that not only did they not know that I was taking something from them, but that they would be eager to give me what I wanted.

"Negotiation, that's the key," she said. "Promise what you must, and keep only those promises that benefit you."

"My mother says that if I tell lies, I will go to Hell," I answered.

"Your mother has no knowledge of statecraft," she retorted. "If the Ducas family knew how to rule, how did your father take over the throne from them?"

"How did he, Grandmother?"

Her stool was near the wall, so she leaned back and considered me thoughtfully. "Did you never hear how that occurred?" she asked. I shook my head. "I did it," she said softly, seeming to look past me now.

"*You* did it, Grandmother?" I asked, astonished. I knew that my father was a great general, that he had started his military career at the age of fourteen, and had never been on the losing side in a battle. I thought that he had merely ordered his soldiers to depose the old emperor, and that they had done so.

"It is not simple to remove an emperor and take his place," my grandmother said. "There is more to it than that. You need friends, allies, supporters. Your father is the

48

greatest general in the world, but like all soldiers, he is used to just taking what he wants. You can't always do that. Sometimes you have to use diplomacy, as I have been teaching you."

"What did you do?" I asked.

"I convinced the Ducas clan to support us, saying that Alexius would marry a Ducas princess—I did not care which one, and your father's fancy was taken with young Irene, so I agreed—and that the Ducases would retain their importance in the court. They had lost the support of the people and were afraid for their very lives. I think the old emperor was actually relieved to have us approach him.

"Once they saw that it was to their advantage to support us, they helped enormously. Your mother's brother-in-law George Palaeologus bribed the guards at the gate of the city, and they opened the gate to your father and his forces."

"No need for a Trojan horse," I said, struck by the similarity to the story told by Homer. How much easier to bribe, make promises, and form alliances, than to besiege a city for years and then be reduced to the stupid trick of a horse filled with soldiers!

"Did the soldiers conquer right away?" I asked.

"Indeed they did. Your father is a great leader. He allowed his soldiers their reward, and they ran through the city, taking whatever they liked, breaking into houses, taking women against their will, filling their pockets with coins, with jewelry, with whatever they could carry. In that way he assured their loyalty."

I was shocked. How could my father have allowed that? I pictured the terrified people running away from leather-clad warriors, knowing that wherever they went, they would encounter more. Surely this was not an honorable way to proceed.

"And did he keep his promises to the Ducas family?"

She gave the odd little snort that I had learned indicated amusement. "He had to keep some," she said. "He married your mother, didn't he?" I nodded. "But I convinced him that it would be foolishness to elevate her to the position of empress. She was only fifteen years old, and I was not besotted with her pretty face, the way your father was, in the way of young men. I could see through her, and I knew that there was little intelligence there, and no spirit."

I shook my head, trying to clear the confusion I felt. Everyone knew that my mother was as strong and wise as she was beautiful. But I did not dare contradict my grandmother, despite my indignation. I felt cold as I remembered the punishments that she had made me suffer in the past. She went on.

"But it seems that some of the people of Constantinople still had a soft spot for the Ducas family, despite their ineffective rule, and they were unhappy when your father excluded her from his coronation. I told him that it was better to keep the people satisfied, and after all, it was no large matter, so he soon had a separate coronation for her. That is why she now has a throne next to your father's, although everyone knows she has not the wit to rule."

A sound at the doorway made me turn around. I felt a

chill when I saw my mother standing there, her face grim. I expected my grandmother to act embarrassed when she realized that my mother had overheard her, but for some reason she did not.

"Do you have a reason for interrupting?" she asked.

"Yes," said my mother in a hard voice. "I wanted to see what you were teaching my daughter. And I am glad I did." She approached me, holding my gaze with her own. I grew warm again, knowing that what my grandmother had said was false, that behind my mother's lovely face was a strong mind and a firm will. I wondered that Grandmother could not see it.

"She did not tell you the complete story, Anna," she said. "Your father did not wish his soldiers to terrorize the city. Indeed, he tried to stop it—"

"If he had tried to stop it, he would have been successful," interrupted my grandmother, but my mother went on as though she hadn't heard her.

"His soldiers were excited at the ease with which they had conquered," she said, "and many of them were from barbarian countries where the victorious side customarily destroys the town and inhabitants they have beaten. They did not speak Greek, and could not understand the orders to cease." She paused.

"I remember that night well," she went on softly. "I was in our villa outside the city for safety, and could hear the shrieks and alarm-bells even from that distance. I could smell the smoke as it rose from burning houses. That whole side of the sky was lit with a deep red glow. I thought it was Hell, that we were all going to burn there forever as punishment for the sins of our soldiers. It was *not* glorious!" she suddenly said vehemently, turning to my grandmother. "War is never glorious!"

My grandmother did not answer.

In a calmer tone, my mother continued. "When order was finally restored, your father had his soldiers confined to quarters for a day to make them calm down. After that, all was peaceful. But your father was not happy. He knew that what had happened was his responsibility as the leader, even though he had tried to stop it, and he confessed the sin to the patriarch. That wise man agreed that your father was guilty, and so was everyone else who had participated. We *all*"—she emphasized the word while glancing at my grandmother, who still sat like a statue—"we all had to fast for forty days, eating only bread, drinking only water. Your father had to wear sackcloth that irritated his skin so that for weeks after the penance had ended I was rubbing it with ointment."

I tried to picture my proud father wearing sackcloth, which I had seen on the bodies of condemned prisoners and the penitent sinners over whom I had to step when entering the church. The image was impossible for me to conjure up.

"But Mother," I said. "Why did Father not want you to be empress?"

A bitter laugh came from her lips as she swung to look at my grandmother, who did not return her gaze. "You mustn't believe everything she tells you," she said. "Your father *did* want me to be empress." A snort from my grandmother. "His mother convinced him that if he had me crowned, the Ducas family would see that as a sign of weakness on his part and would rise in rebellion against him. But out of love for me and out of respect for his word, he delayed only a month before recognizing that he had to do what was right, and had me crowned. Many times he has apologized for not doing so immediately.

"And now, Anna," she continued, "I want you to come with me. Enough studying for one day."

My grandmother rose quickly to her feet. "I have not finished with today's lesson," she said.

"And I say you have," answered my mother.

"The emperor commands that she learn what I have to teach her," was the reply.

"And the empress commands that you cease."

They appeared to be at an impasse.

"Wait," said my grandmother. "Let the child decide. It is, after all, her future that is at stake. Anna, when you are empress you will need to know how to rule. You will also need someone who is experienced in statecraft to guide you. I have knowledge of all areas of rule—war, peace, diplomacy, economy—what do you have to offer?" She wheeled on my mother.

My mother did not hesitate. "I have God's law," she said. "I have compassion, mercy, and justice. And I too know what is expected of a ruler. I, after all, was raised in a palace, not in an Armenian goatherd's tent." Goatherd's tent? I thought in confusion. Grandmother was the daughter of a goatherd? And Armenian? Surely they were barbarians, like the Turks? But I had little time to wonder at what my mother had said.

"Enough," said my grandmother. "Decide, Anna."

I looked from one to the other. My mother's idea of a gentle rule appealed to me. But what good had it done her family? An emperor deposed and exiled in his old age, a city destroyed, churches looted. And if my father was ruling under his mother's advice, should I not follow his example and use her as my teacher too? Surely he, of all people, knew which of them was better at teaching me. My father was a glorious emperor. The Turks were being beaten back farther from our borders every day, so we were told. My father had recently established the largest leper hospital in the world, where ill people were taken care of and given the last rites as they died. New churches with glorious paintings and mosaics in them were rising all over the empire. Surely, if he had to tell a few lies to accomplish all this, if he had to disappoint a few allies, it made for more peace and stability in the long run. Not to mention a stronger hold on the throne.

"I'm sorry, Mother," I said. "I will need my grandmother to help me rule when I become empress."

"What makes you think she will still be alive?" my mother broke in, tears starting from her eyes.

I hadn't thought of that. My grandmother seemed ageless.

"Well, if she isn't, I will need all the more time to learn from her now," I said. "I will happily learn from you, too..." I said desperately as she turned to leave. "Mother," I pleaded, "I want to learn your lessons too!" But she had already disappeared through the door. For a moment I thought of following her, but before I could move, my grandmother's voice stopped me. It was cold, but the note of triumph was unmistakable.

"Now I will tell you about the tactics used by the Normans," she said. I turned and sat down wearily. Her voice went on and on, but I didn't hear a word. Instead, I kept picturing the city of Constantinople in flames, my father in sackcloth, my mother humiliated. But the image of the old Ducas king, whom my father had replaced, reduced to the status of a common man, rose in my mind. I saw him, once the proud leader of millions, riding in a common coach, being borne away to a monastery to live out his life in dreary exile. My stomach churned at the thought. Anything but that, I said to myself, and with an effort drew my attention back to the present.

CHAPTER
SEVEN

My father was coming home. Messengers had arrived on exhausted horses to tell us that the war had been a success and the Turks were for the moment not a problem. But my father did not come with them, and although my mother didn't say so, I knew she was worried at the delay. I, on the other hand, prided myself on my patience. After all, I had waited to be born until he returned from war, hadn't I? I knew he was safe and would be back soon.

Besides, I was too busy to worry. As an eleven-year-old, I was nearly a woman. The woman is the head of the household, and when I was empress, I would have an enormous household to supervise. I would have to make sure there was food for everyone in all the palaces in the imperial compound. I would need to see to it that new servants were properly trained, that livestock was kept in good order, that everyone was properly clothed, and that the children received their education. The health of my family would be in my hands, and although the imperial family had the best physicians in the empire, final responsibility for everyone's health would be mine. I enjoyed medical studies the most, and my cousins soon learned to flee from me when they saw me approaching with bandages, or the box of herbs used to mix up remedies.

And when my husband was out of the city (as Constantine would often be), I would also be in charge of defense of the palace against invaders. I secretly hoped that would happen. I knew I would be good at battle.

Lessons continued with Simon. I think my mother must have spoken to him about her encounter with my grandmother, for suddenly he was dwelling longer than usual on the philosophers and church fathers who said that maintaining one's word is the only way to govern fitly. He also had us read and memorize gruesome stories of war. My favorite book was the *Iliad*, and one day Simon set me a reading assignment from the part where Priam, the king of Troy, went to beg the Greeks for the body of his beloved son, Hector. Hector, with his golden helmet and athletic prowess, reminded me of Constantine, and tears stung my eyes each time I read of his death. Please let Constantine be safe, I prayed silently each time we came to that part.

The Greek Achilles, blinded by his fury over the death

57

of his best friend, Patroclus, killed by Hector, had slain the Trojan hero and mutilated his body by dragging it behind his chariot. I was standing on the table with my back to the doorway, declaiming as Simon had taught me, and had just reached the part where Hector's father pleads for his son's body when I saw Simon's eyes drop and his hands cross submissively on his round stomach. This usually meant that my grandmother had come to take me for private study, so I turned to the door, ready to go, when I saw that instead of her black columnar figure, my mother was standing there, robed in red.

She approached. "And what does this story teach us, children?" she asked. No one spoke, so she answered for us. "Achilles refused to obey the laws of his gods and of man, and he was himself killed. Even in war," she said, emphasizing the last word and looking me in the face, "even in war, there are rules to be followed. A leader must lead honorably."

The others looked bored. What had this to do with them? And the battles in the *Iliad* were glorious to read, despite the talk of rules and leading honorably. My mother looked at me meaningfully once more, then left the room. We returned to our studies, but the episode had lost its fascination for me.

In my rare free time, I returned to some of my childish games. My brain was weary, and as Constantine was with my father he would never know if I helped amuse my sister Maria by playing with her dolls. One day we had avoided the midday sun by going into the Balchernae Palace's inner courtyard. This was our favorite place, since there we were outdoors but still enclosed in the safe walls of the palace.

We were pretending that our dolls were soldiers. Maria was then only eight, so she had to obey me when I told her that her dolls were the barbarians and mine were the Greeks. Remembering my medical lessons, I had torn up tiny scraps of linen to make bandages, and crushed the small grass seeds around us to make medicines for my wounded heroes. My troops were massacring Maria's in vast hordes, and she wanted to provide them with Christian burial. I told her that infidels weren't Christians, but she said, "Mine are," and refused to continue the game until they were properly buried. I gave in and told her that we needed something. Before she could ask what it was, I slipped into the chapel that was near our play area, and took the heavy silver chalice Father Agathos used for the sacramental wine.

Maria's eyes widened when she saw it. "Put it back, Anna!" she said. "What if Mother were to see?"

I knew that my punishment would be swift and sure if we were found out—probably I would have to kneel on the bare stone floor of the church for half a day, saying prayers in penance. My knees ached at the thought. But the added danger just made the chalice more special to me.

"Don't worry," I assured her. "I'll tell her it was my idea. You won't get in any trouble."

I was administering the last rites to the captain of Maria's forces when a sudden rustle of silk told me that our mother was coming through the cloth hanging on the doorway. I hastily picked up the chalice to stuff it in the pouch hanging at my waist. To my horror, it didn't fit, so I whipped my hand behind me and stood with my heart thumping and my head properly bowed, awaiting her.

I looked upward under my eyelashes at my mother. She was accompanied by a barefoot girl somewhat taller than I, whom I had never seen before. The girl was dressed in the garb of a household servant. When my mother drew near, she said, "You may approach, Princesses." We walked to her, heads still down, and kissed her hand. I hoped she would not notice that my left hand was behind my back. I then raised my head and looked at her companion.

A round brown face looked back at me. The muddy brown eyes were unattractive, although they shone with an intelligence that disconcerted me. The girl had long, curly hair that would have benefited from a good brushing. She must be new, I thought, and doesn't know how to keep herself like an imperial slave. She seemed to be about my age, although with barbarians it is often hard to tell. We looked at each other in silence.

"This is your new maid," my mother said. "She is my gift to you."

The maid kept looking at me. The impertinence of her direct gaze made me want to slap her, but I did not like to do so in front of my mother, who believed in treating slaves like people. I wish Grandmother were here, I thought. She would soon have her spirit broken the way it should be.

"She seems untrained," I answered, "but I think I can make her useful."

"She is indeed, as you say, untrained," my mother answered. "You have started learning your new duties. It seemed wise to me to have the two of you learn together. That way you can teach each other."

I felt my cheeks flame hot. A slave teach *me*! I knew what my grandmother would say if she heard such a thing: "A Comnenus to be taught by a slave, indeed! Only a Ducas would find such a thing suitable."

"How could *she* help me, Mother?" I asked, my voice rising high in protest.

"You are no longer a child, Anna," she said gently. "You will find that you will need someone trustworthy, who is not involved in politics, in whom you can confide. If this girl proves worthy of your trust, perhaps she will be that one. She has no stake in what our families do. Besides, you need to learn how to train a maid. You will soon ally the Comnenus and Ducas families and will have a large staff to handle."

She looked me full in the face, smiling. I knew she was proud of the blood of her Ducas family, which had been noble while most of my father's family—I was forced to admit—were merely wealthy landowners.

"Don't play too long in the heat," my mother said. "Give me a kiss before I return to my chamber."

My face felt hot as I realized the impossibility of embracing my mother as she expected. My new maid was watching me, her head on one side, and she suddenly approached me.

"Your Grace has gotten dirty," she said with a thick accent. "You don't want to soil your mother's lovely robe."

She brushed off the dust on my skirt as she walked around me, and I felt her lightly remove the chalice from my hand. She returned to her original place, her hand hidden in the folds of her dress. As I kissed my mother's cheek, I saw the girl slip the chalice into her pocket, which being a servant's was much larger than the dainty pouch I wore at my waist.

Suddenly I jumped at a noise from outside the palace. Heralds were shouting, trumpets were blaring. It didn't sound like an attack, but still Maria and I looked at my mother for reassurance. She was staring in the same direction I was, her brow furrowed, her hand to her throat.

"Go inside, Princesses," she said. She hastened back through the door.

The three of us stood still, heads bowed, hands properly clasped, until we heard the cloth hanging swing shut. Then I turned to the girl. There was a twinkle in her eye and I could tell that she was trying to repress a grin. I pretended not to notice it.

"Why did you do that?" I asked. She shrugged. "How did you know I was hiding that chalice?" I persisted.

"You looked the way my little sister did when she kept a kitten that my father had told her to take to the barn," she answered. "Only, of course, your clothes are much more elegant."

She was getting too familiar, although she had not actually said anything offensive.

"What is your name?" I asked her.

"Your mother tells me that my name is now Sophia," she answered.

62

"Whose household did you serve before you came here?"

Finally, I had managed to remove the smile from her face, although I had no idea how I had done it. I was pleased to see that her expression was properly submissive now. I leaned closer to look at her. Her lips were clamped tight together and her cheeks were red. They looked hot.

At last she answered, "I did not serve in a household. I lived with my mother and father and brothers and little sister in a village far from Constantinople."

"Oh-ho," I said. "Now I see. You're a Turk!"

She did not say anything, which was answer enough. Turks were constantly trying to invade the empire. They were always quickly subdued by the imperial forces, and any survivors of the battles were of course enslaved.

"Where is your little sister now, and the rest of your family?"

No answer. Then, "Dead. Or sold into slavery, like me," she said. "Most of my village was killed. The man I was to marry—I think I saw him being led off the day I was found in the woods. But I don't know about anyone else."

I tried to picture Constantine Ducas being led off in chains, but couldn't succeed in seeing his proud form bent in submission. An image of Hector's mutilated body returned to me once more, and I shuddered.

CHAPTER
EIGHT

The maid was still staring at me with curious brown eyes. "What is it?" I asked impatiently.

"Are you really a princess?" she asked.

"I am," I answered, trying to hide my pride at her obvious awe. "I am the daughter of Emperor Alexius Comnenus, who conquered the empire when he was only twenty-four. And when I am older, in a year or two, I will marry Constantine Ducas, a relative of the emperor my father deposed. I haven't yet decided whether I will let him be emperor or not. In either case, I will then be empress."

"I too am betrothed," broke in the girl eagerly. "I am to marry the son of our neighbor, Malik. He is older than

I, but very kind, and when he finds me, we will wed, and go live with his brother in the mountains——"

"What do I care about your peasant alliances?" I burst out, astonished that she was addressing me so familiarly. "Do you dare compare this farmer's son to Constantine Ducas? Do you not know that one day I will be ruling the entire empire while you dream of living with your brother-in-law? And what makes you think you will be released from your servitude to marry?"

Her face clouded over, but she wore a resolute expression. "I just know it will happen," she said. "And how do you know that someday you will rule all these lands? Other kings have had their thrones taken away from them, or so I hear. And if you do rule, how will you know what to do?"

Despite my grandmother's reassurances, I still felt uneasy at the thought of governing the vast Byzantine Empire. But I hid my feelings and answered as casually as I could, "I have already learned much about statesmanship, and will have many advisors to help me. My grandmother, Anna Dalassena, is so trusted by my father that when he is away she rules in his place. And she will help me."

"How can someone help the empress?" asked the girl.

"Why—she will tell me what to do. And I will do it," I said. It seemed obvious.

"Then won't she really be the empress, and not you?" persisted Sophia.

I did not like the direction this conversation was taking. Who was this infidel, this slave, this representative of a conquered race, to be questioning me? And what did she mean by that question? Surely if I were sitting on the throne and if it were up to me to follow or not to follow the advice given me, I would still be the ruler. My grandmother would just be my advisor, as she was for my father. My mother, I had convinced myself, was wrong. My father made up his own mind, and he merely took his mother's advice because it made the most sense. I would do the same, and if I didn't like what she said, I would do something else.

"Enough chatter," I said. "Leave now, and take my sister with you."

"Where do you want me to put this?" Sophia said, indicating her pocket. I had forgotten the chalice. I made up my mind to deal with it as quickly as possible to avoid detection.

"I'll take it," I said. "You're not allowed to go where it belongs."

She handed me the chalice, then stood waiting for further orders.

"You are dismissed," I said. "Take Maria to our chamber. And girl—you are to call me Your Majesty, not Your Grace."

Sophia nodded as if this did not concern her greatly, and reached down to Maria. Before I could stop her, Maria had slipped her small white hand into the thin brown one and went trotting off toward the women's side of the palace. It was not strictly proper for the two of them to be touching, but Maria was still child enough that I supposed it was all right. More important at this moment was my mission of returning the chalice to its proper place in the chapel.

I walked quickly through the corridor and slipped through the chapel's open door. I stood still for a moment, allowing my eyes to get accustomed to the darkness, resting my hand on the cold stone. It was a short run down the aisle to put the chalice back in its case. But before I could take even one step, I heard angry voices coming from the area near the altar, exactly where I had to go myself. Panicked but suddenly curious, I slipped silently behind a tapestry and listened, trying not to sneeze as the dusty fabric pressed against my face. I wanted to see who it was that dared violate the sanctity of the chapel.

At first I could make out only enough to recognize the voices. It was my mother and—could it be?—my father! I almost leaped out from my hiding place until I remembered the chalice I held. At all costs, I wanted to avoid being punished for having borrowed it. So despite my eagerness to see him again, I stayed where I was, and listened.

As my parents talked, they appeared to forget that they were in a holy sanctuary, and their voices rose with anger. I shrank back farther behind the tapestry, desperate now to avoid detection.

"A fine welcome!" my father was saying. "I have been away for nearly a year, and the first thing you tell me after thanking God for my safe return is that my mother must go!"

"Husband . . ." My mother's voice was more pleading than angry, although I recognized a determination in her tone. "If you knew what she was doing, how she was turning our own daughter against us—"

"Turning which daughter against us? Little Maria?" I almost laughed at the thought of my grandmother having any interest at all in my little sister. But my mother's voice held no humor as she replied.

"Anna, our firstborn, your heir—she is becoming hard and cold like your mother, she thinks only of the glory of her future—"

"And it is about time she thought of that, rather than of the studies that that silly little eunuch sets her."

"Simon is not silly, husband, and he is an able tutor. Even your mother admits that the children are better schooled than any she has seen elsewhere. But we were not talking of Simon; we were talking of the way your mother—"

"And I find it hard to believe what you are telling me. I left her in charge of the empire while I was at war, and from all reports things have been running smoothly. Anna is growing up, wife, and it is time she learns what her future holds."

"Her future? Is that all you can think of? And even if it is, what kind of ruler will she be if that harpy squeezes the goodness, the kindness out of her?"

I could tell from the scraping sound that my father had stood up, pushing his chair out from under him. When he spoke next, his voice was cold.

"Her Imperial Majesty Anna Dalassena is not a harpy. If anyone but you had referred to her in such a way, I would have him put to death. You must reflect how much of your hatred toward her goes back to the past, when she tried to convince me not to marry a Ducas, and then not to have you crowned queen, but kept as a secondary wife. That is all long past."

A little laugh, with no humor in it, escaped from my mother. "*Long* past, you say? I did not know that I was allowed to resent her actions for only a limited time. But as you say, this is in the past. What she is doing to the princess is in the present. You must see our daughter, and judge for yourself."

"I intend to do that, madam," said my father. "Let me bathe and rest from my journey, and then after a meal, you will bring the children to me. I will, as you suggest, judge for myself."

I heard him leave the chapel, and then such a long silence fell that I thought my mother must have slipped out unheard by me. But then I heard a heavy sigh, the rustle of silk, and the sound of her feet moving quickly down the aisle toward the door. As soon as she had left, I remembered the chalice. Thank God they had not noticed its absence! I slipped in and placed the chalice as near to its accustomed place as I could in my haste, not bothering to open its wooden case. Let them wonder why it was out; no one had any reason to think I had been in there.

I turned to flee. But as I spun around I caught sight of the embroidered altar cloth, which hung over the high table at which Father Agathos performed the services. The cloth seemed to be bulging in an odd way. I froze as my mind raced for an explanation. Was someone there? But who would hide under the altar? As I stared, the cloth moved a little. But there was no wind in the closed room. The thought came to me that a demon was waiting for me to get near, so he could pounce and bear me to Hell for my theft. I felt frozen, but I forced myself to back slowly away, keeping my gaze fixed on the cloth (which had not moved again), until I nearly stumbled over the threshold of the door as the back of my heel hit it. Then I turned, and ran as fast as I could through the courtyard and back into the door that led to my bedchamber.

CHAPTER NINE

stopped for a moment to catch my breath, pressing flat against the wall to avoid the people hurrying through the halls. All was bustle and confusion; I could tell that a great feast was being prepared. Already the smell of roasting meats and vegetables sizzling in oil wafted from the kitchens. People were shouting orders, slaves were running to obey them. Maids bearing heavy buckets of hot water and thick towels hastened past to prepare baths for the weary travelers. A pair of long-bearded priests hurried past me, bearing incense and fine cloths; I realized that they were heading toward the chapel to prepare a Mass of thanksgiving so that we all could give thanks publicly for my father's safe return. I

sent up my own prayer of thanksgiving that I had been successful in returning the chalice to its proper place before they arrived there.

I hoped to find peace to reflect on what I had heard in the chapel when I entered my room, but as soon as she caught sight of me, Sophia grabbed my arm and pulled me in. "Where have you been?" she demanded.

"Sophia..." I started automatically to reprimand her for her familiarity, but stopped. It seemed, after all, a losing battle, and in any case, she was not listening to me.

"Your father has returned from the war," she said, and I tried to look surprised. Fortunately, no one was paying much attention to me. Maria was already propped up on a high stool while her maid endeavored to coax her fine red hair into some kind of order, and before I knew what was happening, Sophia had pushed me down into a chair and was pulling the combs and ribbons out of my own black hair. She handed me a mirror, fresh ribbons, and pins, commanded, "Hold these!" and started brushing the snarls out my hair, muttering to herself at the mess she was finding there.

"If you do not look proper at the reception, it will be I who takes the blame, and I who receive the whipping. Where have you been?"

I didn't answer, merely squirmed away as her too-harsh treatment yanked my scalp.

"Hold still!" she said. Her deft fingers found the source of the knot she was working on, and quickly smoothed it out. Finally the brush finished its work, but not before my head was burning. Sophia started making the tiny braids all over my head that my mother found most suitable for her daughters, weaving gold beads and bright ribbons in among the strands. Until we were married, we would of course wear our hair down, and it was a challenge for Sophia and Dora, Maria's maid, to find hairstyles ornate enough to set us apart from the common women, without having recourse to the knots and coils that married women could use.

Now that the tangles were out, the feel of Sophia's fingers began to be soothing, and I leaned back against her and closed my eyes. Seeing how still I was, she stopped scolding and continued her work, occasionally pushing me forward, away from her, to work on my back hair.

Finally, silence to reflect. I uncomfortably recalled what I had heard, and knew that I could never ask about it without giving away my presence in the chapel. What had my mother been talking about? My grandmother was not teaching me anything unseemly. Indeed, she was even more strict and rigid than my mother herself, and certainly more proper than Simon, with his scandalous tales of the old gods. She was teaching me the arts of diplomacy, leadership, finance—certainly all skills that I would need in the future. I still did not understand why my mother objected to these studies.

And meanwhile, I was continuing my lessons with Simon. I was easily the best reader in the school, and could memorize long passages from both the Bible and pagan writers. My mathematical skills were good, and I loved to study the orderly, predictable rhythms of the stars when

Simon would wake us all up late at night and take us out on the battlements to watch the heavens in their dance.

I had heard of the bad blood between Anna Dalassena and the Ducas family, but had always thought that my mother was somehow exempt from that hatred, being her daughter-in-law and the mother of the future ruler. I squirmed again as I realized that the discomfort I always felt when in the presence of the two of them together was more than just the lack of ease I experienced in my grandmother's presence. There obviously was a deep dislike—even hatred—there, and it made for a tension that I had felt, even while not understanding its source.

My squirming brought another rebuke from Sophia. "Do you not see how your sister sits so still that Dora is almost through with her hair?"

I glanced sidelong at Maria, who indeed was sitting with her usual serenity. She smiled at me, then turned her eyes in Sophia's direction and made a mocking scowl, imitating Sophia's displeased countenance. Without moving her head, she stretched out a hand in my direction, and I clasped it, glad that she had the forbearance not to appear smug at being praised while I was being scolded. And so we sat, her small hand in mine, until both of us were declared fit to be robed.

We stood, happy to be released from our cramped postures, and stretched out our arms for the sleeves of our gowns. Maria's pale blue silk went on first, making her blue eyes sparkle and her hair appear even brighter than it already was. As Dora knelt to fasten Maria's white slippers, Sophia lifted a new robe over my head. It too was blue, but of a darker hue than my sister's, and around the border was an elaborate design in deep purple.

Startled, I held Sophia off for a moment. "Where did this come from?" I asked. "I am not allowed to wear purple, Sophia; even a Turk must know that. Only the emperor and empress may wear purple."

"Your grandmother brought it in after she heard that your father had arrived. It is by her order that you wear it," answered Sophia, ignoring my restraining hand and pulling the robe over my arms and then my head. She spun me around and started fastening the ribbons that held the robe together in the back, while Dora, finished with Maria, slipped deep blue slippers onto my feet. These were new too, and the tiny buttons up the side were also purple.

The robe fit perfectly, and was of a heavier silk than I was accustomed to wearing. I liked the feel of it as I took a tentative step, then turned to face Maria. Her pretty eyes were wide, and her mouth hung open. "Oh, sister," she breathed. "You look . . . you look . . ." She couldn't finish, but Dora did.

"You look just like your father," she said. Maria nodded in wordless agreement. I wished that I had a mirror larger than the small silver one I held in my hand, but before I could think of how to see my entire form at once, the hanging swung open and our grandmother appeared.

"Let me see the imperial princesses in their finery," she said. She looked Maria up and down, not smiling. "A pretty little thing, you are," she said in a tone of dismissal. "Like your mother. Like a Ducas." Again that tone of contempt as she said the name. Maria didn't answer, but I could see that she was fighting back tears. Grandmother turned from her, as though my sister was not worthy of further comment, and looked at me. This time satisfaction spread over her angular features.

"A Comnenus," she said. She made a twirling motion with her finger to tell me to turn around, which I did, slowly, holding my head as high as I could to increase my height. "But one thing is missing. You are a woman now," she said, drawing a folded cloth from her pocket and approaching me.

I saw that what she held was a veil. "Turn around," she commanded, and I did so, then felt the silk flutter over my face, covering me from the nose to the chin, as she looped the slender cords over my ears and tied them at the back of my head. "Face me again," she said. I did so. The fine cloth felt cool on my face, and moved in and out slightly as I breathed. I realized what an advantage the veil would be in disguising my emotions.

"A true Comnenus," Grandmother said again. "He will be pleased." No need to ask who "he" was, for at that moment we heard the trumpeters from the far end of the palace announce my father's arrival in his throne room. "Come," my grandmother said, extending her thin hand to me. Clutching my fingers in hers, she hastened from the room, leaving Maria to follow, small and forgotten, in our wake.

In a few moments we arrived at the door, the purple hanging with its gold tassels pulled back and secured against the side, the guards in their smart imperial livery

76

standing straight at attention. Quickly Grandmother adjusted my clothes, and as I hung back, trying to delay the inevitable entry, she gave me an impatient push. "Go in," she snapped. "And don't forget your manners!"

I took a deep breath, then started toward the throne, watching my blue and purple slippers flash, flash, flash, against the stones. The familiar patterns of the floor repeated themselves until I knew that I was in front of my father. I stretched out flat, burying my face in my hands, waiting for him to tell me to rise. How would he appear? I wondered. It had been almost a year since I had seen him. I knew I had changed, but I hoped that he had not.

I did not have long to wait. Rather than hearing his voice telling me to rise, it was his hands I felt on my upper arms—his hard, callused palms scraping and catching on the fine material, lifting me to my feet, the smell of his leather boots filling my nostrils—and finally I dared to look up, and there he was, Alexius Comnenus, emperor of the Byzantines, conqueror of the Turks, his beard a little more gray, perhaps, his face a little more lined, but still my father, home from the war.

CHAPTER
TEN

I murmured a dazed welcome as he pressed his hand on top of my head, blessing me. "Daughter Anna," he said, and my heart sank, sure that I was about to be interrogated about my grandmother and what I was learning from her. Fortunately, it was not to be yet, but I did not have the chance to relax, for another interrogation was in store for me. My father placed his hand lightly under my chin and tilted my head up. He frowned a little. "A veil?" he said. He turned to my mother. "Surely she is not old enough. She is but—how old are you, child?"

"She is almost twelve," my mother answered. "And I agree with you, she is too young to be wearing a veil. I don't even know where she got it from."

"She got it from me," said my grandmother, so smoothly that it seemed as though she had been waiting for the question. "At her age I had already been veiled for two years. She is not a Ducas, but a Comnenus, and she must behave accordingly."

I dared not look at my mother, and she did not reply. My father sighed and passed his hand over his face. He suddenly looked weary, and I realized how fatigued he must be from the journey. After all, he must have been riding hard to come home again and see us all. But he seemed to pull himself more erect, and once more turned his smile in my direction.

"You have grown, child," he said, "and look ready to step into my throne. Surely that is not purple you are wearing on your gown?" He looked amused rather than angry, although I knew how strictly he observed rules governing who should wear what color and what style.

"I did not know it had purple on it until I was ready to put it on," I said, my voice scarcely rising above a whisper.

"Ah, so it is a new robe?" he asked. I nodded. He turned to my mother. "And which of our weaving-women decided to add purple to the border?" he asked. Before she could answer, my grandmother did so.

"It was a gift from me, Alexius," she said. "I told the slave to make it deep blue with red embroidery around the edges. Evidently she thought that purple would be a better color. She is not of our race, my son, and does not know the significance we place on imperial purple. I have already had the woman flogged for her mistake."

My father made a face. I knew how much he disliked

unnecessary punishment. "Surely," he said, "if the slave did not know of her misdeed beforehand, a reprimand would have sufficed."

My grandmother's expression did not change, although I thought I noted a touch of coldness in her voice when she replied. "That is not the way of the Comneni, Your Majesty. A slave who willfully disobeys must be punished so that others do not think we are soft. I had told her to use red, and she used purple. Next time, she will think twice before taking it upon herself to disobey my order."

As always, my father did not contradict his mother, although I knew that he disapproved of beating slaves for such small reasons. Instead, he sighed and turned to Maria, who had not been long to follow me in. He blessed her in her turn, exclaimed over how she had grown, and how much she resembled our mother. She looked terrified as she tried to answer him, and suddenly my heart went out to my little sister, who was so obviously trying to be brave. She looked relieved when her blessing was accomplished and she moved next to me as we lined up next to my mother. We dared not hold hands in so public an assembly, but I sidled close to her, and under the cover of our long robes I pressed the toe of my slipper reassuringly on her foot. She glanced up a little at me, and a tiny smile moved across her lips.

Finally it was John's turn. I leaned forward a little, as I had not seen him close up in months, although I had heard stories of his legendary tantrums, his refusals to wear appropriate clothes, and of course his continued absence from the schoolroom. He was taller, I saw, although still short for a six-year-old. But for once, it appeared, the nurse had had no difficulty in getting him to wear proper dress, or even to behave correctly. He stood in front of our father, his head bowed with respect, hands clasped in front of him. What a little gentleman, I thought, and glanced sidelong at Maria. She was staring at the boy in frank astonishment.

"My son," said our father. John approached. Our father must surely be nearly a stranger to him now, and I was curious to see how the boy would respond. John approached in a most seemly manner, head held low, humility oozing from every pore. I had never seen him so proper. Nor had anyone else, and I saw amazement on everyone's features. John knelt at my father's feet, and as my father pressed his hand on the boy's head in blessing, John looked up at him and threw himself in the emperor's arms, crying out, "I missed you so!"

Taken aback by this display of emotion, my father patted John awkwardly on the back, looking around desperately for someone to help him. John's nurse came to the rescue, pulling the little boy, sobbing now, off my father. "My apologies, sire," she said, bowing low. "We have been inclined to spoil him during your absence, and have neglected to school him sufficiently in his behavior toward his elders."

"No matter," said my father. "I am more pleased than otherwise." He looked John up and down. "So, my son, how has it been faring with you? Are you making progress in your studies?"

"Oh, yes, Father," said John. "Master Simon is most

pleased with my progress." I felt my jaw drop open, and saw that Maria was gaping too. Did he not care that we all knew he was lying, or was he counting on our unwillingness to displease our father by exposing the lie to keep us silent? I clenched my teeth to keep from blurting out the truth.

"And do you help your mother while I am away? You are my son, and must be the man when I am not here."

"Yes, Father," he said, and again I had to struggle to hide my disgust at his barefaced lies. Far from being a help, John made everyone work even harder trying to keep him satisfied and not causing trouble with his temper. But my father seemed to believe him, and even our grandmother nodded approval.

"Good, good," my father said, smiling again. "You may go now and join the others." John approached us, lifting his face in my direction to find his proper spot. I noticed that despite his apparent sobbing a moment before, John's face was completely dry of tears, and no redness marred his eyes. Little hypocrite, I thought with contempt. He is no more moved at our father's homecoming than he would be at a servant's return. As he took his place next to Maria, I could feel her shift her weight slightly in my direction, as though to avoid contact with our brother. Good, I thought. So she doesn't like him either. The thought cheered me, I know not why. I think the realization made me feel less alone.

My father seemed determined to make everyone happy, and he started by showing us the treasures he had brought back from his travels. Surrounded by his advisors, both those he had taken with him and those who had remained behind to help my grandmother govern, he ordered box after box brought forward and opened. Fabrics, both silk and of other glowing materials, in many glittering colors, were presented to our dazzled eyes. Painted pictures, some enclosed in precious golden frames, ivory figurines, silver buckles, gold earrings, jeweled necklaces—after a while I felt drunk with the sight. Slaves, some of regal bearing and proud faces, others with beaten-down expressions and wilting postures, were paraded in front of us. Small boxes of precious spices were thrown open until the very air seemed heavy with the scents.

To my mother he presented a gold and crystal box, containing a tiny piece of something yellow. "Can you guess what it is, wife?" he asked.

"I hardly d-d-dare hope . . ." she stammered.

"Yes," he replied. "It is a piece of the finger bone of St. Irene, your patroness." Mother dropped to her knees and pressed her lips to the front of the reliquary. The small church of St. Irene was dear to her heart, being dedicated not only to the saint for whom she was named, but also to peace. I knew how she longed for the wars with the Turks to end so that my father would stay home.

Her trembling hands threatened to drop the precious fragment, so my father signaled to Father Agathos to bear it away. He did so with great reverence.

To Maria my father gave a chessboard of inlaid precious woods and stones, with intricately carved ivory pieces. John's gift was a tiny white pony with a splendid saddle, which my father said he had captured from a Turkish chieftain who kept it in his tent, like a pet. And to me he gave a gorgeous parrot, green, gold, and red. I was frightened of its beak and odd, wrinkled claws, but also intrigued by its bright colors, its exotic face, and the words it uttered in a crackly voice. I couldn't understand its speech, but my father said it was Turkish, and that the bird was asking me for a treat. One of the servants handed me a grape, and I offered it in the parrot's direction. He took it with a surprisingly gentle claw, ate it, and then spoke again.

"He said, 'Thank you,'" my father translated. I was enchanted. Many people had chessboards like Maria's, and I already had a pony that was prettier than John's, but no one had a talking bird.

After we had all exclaimed over our gifts, and they had been removed by the servants, my father dismissed us. As we children all turned to leave, my father said, "But you stay, Princess Anna."

I longed so to keep walking, to pretend I had not heard, but I knew that it was useless. I retraced my steps, stopping in front of the throne, and wondered if I should make my bow to the floor again. But my father was descending the platform, and took me by the hand to a small stool normally occupied by one of his counselors. He sat on another stool next to mine.

"Have you missed me too?" he asked, continuing to hold my hand.

"Of course, Father," I said. Tears rose to my eyes. I had struggled so hard to maintain my dignity and treat him with respect, successfully fighting the urge to leap into his lap as I had done when a child, and now he thought that I was being formal only because I had not missed him, whereas John's false outburst was seen as true love. No matter what I did, it seemed to be wrong.

But he did not appear to notice my tears. "Have you missed anyone else?" he asked. I looked at him, confused. Who could he mean? But without turning around, he put his hand behind him and beckoned with a finger. Out of the throng of men stepped a tall athletic figure, crowned with glorious golden hair.

It was Constantine Ducas, and he was smiling at me. He had broadened during the year away, and looked more like a man than like the slender youth he had been when he left. His face bore a new scar, but it did not detract from his beauty, merely made him appear a more seasoned veteran than an untried novice.

"Your betrothed acquitted himself well," my father said, "and bears with him even now the marks of his valor."

Constantine suddenly laughed, a merry sound that dispelled much of the tension I had been feeling. "This scar was not made by a sword-cut, Princess," he said, touching the mark where it ran around his jawbone. "Nothing so exciting. I was unhorsed during our first campaign, and as I fell, I scraped my face on the ornaments on my saddle. From then on, I assure you I rode with a saddle as plain as any used by our humblest knight!"

"Ah, but he slew many a Turk after that battle," my father said.

"How many Turks were there?" I asked. Both men laughed, looking at each other.

"Numbers impossible to count," my father said. "Some were valiant soldiers, others were as cowardly as their infidel souls would make them. But are you interested in warfare?"

"Oh, yes," I said, my eagerness making me forget to be dignified. "I want to know what kind of battle-engines you used, and how the campaigns were waged, and what were the terms of surrender——" I stopped short, afraid that Constantine would laugh at my eagerness. But instead, he approached, his face serious again. He knelt next to me, so that despite his height his head was nearly at a level with mine as I sat on my stool.

"I am glad you are interested in these things," he said, "and when we have rested I will tell you all you wish to know. Accompanied by a proper chaperone, of course," he added hastily, and I felt myself blush as I realized that I had been imagining speaking with him alone.

Seeing my confusion, perhaps, my father hastily intervened. "Why don't you show us what else you have learned, Princess, by checking on the progress of the feast while we go to our rooms and prepare ourselves to dine?"

I rose to my feet, and they did too. I bowed to my father, scarcely dared to glance at Constantine, and walked as quickly as I could out of the throne room. I didn't slow down until I had turned enough corners to make sure that no one could see me, and then I leaned against the wall and pressed my hand to my chest, feeling my heart pounding and my breath coming in short gasps. Had I acted like a fool? Would he think me a silly child, one not yet old enough to wear the veil, just as my father had?

When I had regained my composure, I continued on my way to the kitchen. It was familiar territory to me, as my mother had been instructing me in the proper methods of supervising the meals. A palace was just a large house, she reminded me, and the mistress of the house must be in charge of making sure the larders were full, and that delicious and wholesome food was available to all who hungered.

I passed near a garbage heap outside one of the minor kitchens, and my eye was caught by a flash of green and gold on top of it. I stopped and looked more closely. It was my parrot, the one my father had brought back for me, and it lay there dead, its neck wrung. Its eyes were already glazing over. As I stared in horrified disbelief, a slave passed nearby and saw me staring.

"That bird bit the little prince, Your Majesty," he said. "It drew blood and made him scream, and as soon as he could draw breath again, he ordered it killed. Dirty beast, and not big enough to eat. If you'll excuse me, I have my work to do." He passed on through the door as I stared at the silent bird, my errand forgotten.

CHAPTER
ELEVEN

The feast was glorious. There were musicians, jugglers, and storytellers. Everyone was in a happy mood at the return of the warriors, and the tales my father and the other men were telling must have been uproariously funny, to judge from the reaction of their companions. John was taking his place at the men's table for the first time. I glared at him, wishing I could have him punished for killing my parrot. But I knew that no one would listen to me. Anyone, even an animal, that harmed a member of the imperial family, had to be dealt with severely. The parrot had been executed for the crime of treason.

Since the men and women sat at different tables, we women could remove our veils as we ate. I was glad of this, for I had no practice in eating veiled, and did not want to do it for the first time at such a banquet. The food was delicious; all my father's favorite savory dishes were served. The spices made me thirsty, and I drank more wine than I was used to. My mother was so occupied with attending to my father's needs, sending platters of special dishes to his table, bidding servants to refill his glass when it was only half empty, that she did not notice how much drink I consumed.

The wine made the evening pass more quickly. But when a platter of roasted peacock was brought out, its tail arranged around its steaming body in a glowing display of green and gold feathers, I suddenly saw again the corpse of my parrot lying on the rubbish heap. A wave of nausea hit me, and I slipped from the table.

I knew that my absence would be noted if I stayed away for long, so instead of returning to my chamber to lie down, I stepped out the nearest doorway into the courtyard to breathe some fresh air. I leaned my forehead against a cool stone column, and stayed that way until my breathing slowed and my stomach settled. The sweet smell of the flowers and herbs growing in the small space cleared my head and I straightened up, gathering the courage to enter the noisy, hot room again. I had thought I was alone, so I jumped when a voice behind me said, "Are you unwell, Princess?"

Whirling around, I saw Constantine Ducas sitting on a stone bench not three yards away. Hurriedly I adjusted my veil to cover my mouth and chin again, and looked around to see if anyone else was in sight. Nobody, to my relief.

He must have read my mind, for he said, "I know it is not really proper for us to be here together, but I don't think anyone else will follow us. They are enjoying themselves too much."

As if to confirm his words, a burst of laughter flew out the door. I relaxed a little. "What are you doing out here, Cousin?" I asked. I felt too shy to use any other name.

"All the noise and the food . . ." He shook his head. "It was too strong a contrast with the way I have been living recently, camping out in a tent, eating what we could find. I needed to come out and remind myself that there was still an outer world, still a sky with stars." I looked up at the familiar constellations as he said that. I felt him move nearer, and quickly took a step back. He stopped immediately.

"Don't worry," he said. "It is not really improper for us to spend a few minutes alone together. We are, after all, betrothed, and have been for a long time. Indeed, our betrothal is one of my earliest memories."

"*I* don't remember it," I said, wondering.

"Of course you don't," he said with a grin. "You were an infant in your cradle. They led me up to where you lay, and told me that someday you and I would wed, and at that moment you started crying. Everyone laughed, and I started crying too. My nurse gave me a piece of sugar to suck on. So you see, our first meeting was sweet, for me at least." I nodded, not knowing what to say. I was embarrassed at the story, even though I knew that crying is normal for babies.

"I hope," he said in a more serious voice, "I hope,

90

Princess Anna, that the thought of our engagement does not displease you now."

"Oh, no—" I started to say, but my voice came out in a croak. I paused and started over, hoping he hadn't noticed. "Oh, no, Prince Constantine, the thought is most pleasing. I can think of no one I would rather wed."

"Good," said he, still keeping a careful distance. "Now, perhaps, we had better return to the feast. Engaged couples are notorious for sneaking off on their own, and we don't want anyone to think that we're doing anything—"

"No, no," I said hastily, not waiting for him to finish. I gathered up my long skirts and moved through the open doorway. I slipped as quietly as I could into my seat, and took a sip of wine, hoping to slow the beating of my heart. Constantine, I saw, had also regained his seat, and was carefully, or so it appeared, avoiding looking in my direction.

Then I noticed that John's place was empty. But it did not remain so for long. He came in through the same door Constantine and I had used. My heart sank. Had that monkey been out there with us? He did not look at me, but instead went straight to our father, and whispered something in his ear. My father appeared to ask him a question, and John nodded vigorously. Then my father glanced over at me, and in Constantine's direction, before pointing to John's empty seat. John nodded again, and returned to where he had been sitting, shooting me a smug smile as he did so. I saw that his hand was bandaged. I wish my parrot had bitten his finger all the way off, I thought savagely.

My appetite gone for good now, I sat at the table and watched as course after course was laid out, served, and removed. The best I could manage was to shift the food around to make it look as though I had eaten some. Voices around me rose and fell in song. The din was deafening.

I was sickened at the thought that at any moment my father might call me up to his table and ask me what had transpired outside. But perhaps I would escape, as the meal was ending. The musicians made a final flourish of their instruments, the acrobat turned one last handspring out the door, and my father and mother rose, he at the head of the men's table, she at the women's.

"Friends and family!" called out my father. "Thank you for your attendance at this banquet. All of us are most heartily glad to be back. Only some seem more glad than others. Constantine!" he called. My betrothed stepped forward, looking confused. He bowed to my father, then looked up expectantly.

"We missed you for a long time at the table," went on my father. "Where did you disappear to?"

Everyone was silent, and all except me (and John, I was by now sickeningly sure) must have wondered what he was talking about.

Constantine made a gesture with his hands as though to dismiss the question. "I wished to go to the ah—ah—" he stumbled.

"Oh, did you?" my father said. "Well, you must have gotten confused, because the door to the ah—ah—is over there, and you were seen coming in *this* door. Surely, Constantine, you know that we are no longer on campaign, and there are proper places for doing these things!"

By now everyone knew my father was joking, and they

were laughing at the young man's confusion. All except me. My father then picked little John up and stood him on the table in front of him. "Tell us what you heard," he commanded, and the little imp turned to face the company, his piercing voice, mocking mine and Constantine's, "Our first meeting was sweet for me, Princess Anna— Oh, Prince Constantine, I can think of no one I would rather wed."

Laughter erupted once more. Even Constantine appeared not to be offended at being mocked, but joined in the merriment, grabbing at my brother, tickling him and saying, "You little fiend! Where were you hiding?"

The only two faces I could see that were not laughing were those of my mother, who looked imploringly at me, and my grandmother, who stood apart, grimly surveying the scene. I tried my best to join in the mirth, but with the tears starting from my eyes, it was impossible to feign a laugh without allowing a sob to escape from my throat.

Finally, wiping his eyes, my father spoke over the crowd again. "Enough, enough, we are embarrassing them! Let us all retire for the night. Your Majesty?"

My mother still looking at me, did not answer. My father repeated, "Your Majesty?" and she started as though awakened from a dream, put her veil back over her face, and went toward him at the men's table. Hand in hand they went out the door. I longed to follow on their heels, but escape was not to prove so easy. Before I could leave I had to put up with the jokes of all who passed, and it was not until the crowd had thinned enough to let me out that I fled, seeking the sanctuary of my bedchamber.

Thank Heaven, it was empty but for Maria. I flung myself on my bed and let go of the sobs that I had been holding in ever since my father had first addressed Constantine. Maria sat by my side, stroking my hair, making soothing noises. After I had cried myself silent, I lay face-down, exhausted. I heard footsteps, and Maria rose from the bed. Raising myself up on one elbow, I saw her making the usual bow to our mother. I didn't bother to do the same, certain that she wasn't going to scold me for lack of respect. And she did not, but took Maria's place, sitting next to me on the bed.

"Anna," she said, "Anna, my darling, you must learn to relax your dignity a little."

"Relax my dignity, Mother?" I said, starting up with indignation. "You ask me to stand by in peace while I am mocked?"

"But, Anna," she said, "that kind of teasing is common with betrothed couples. I saw how much you were suffering and felt for you, but it is something you must grow accustomed to. You won't be married for several more years, and it is bound to happen again."

"Father wasn't trying to make you sad, Anna," Maria said, her little face looking worried.

"I know, Maria." I was too exhausted to tell her how humiliated I had been. I wished they would both leave me alone, and let Sophia undress me so I could sleep.

"Then why are you crying?"

Before I could explain, an answer came from the doorway.

"She is crying from shame," said a cold voice. I looked

up. There stood Anna Dalassena, her face stern, her long hand gripping the door frame.

"She has not behaved like a princess," continued my grandmother, stepping into the chamber. "She has not behaved like a Comnenus. She has behaved like a Ducas, like a silly, weak girl, and she knows she has degraded herself by so doing."

"Enough," said my mother coldly. "The child has suffered enough tonight."

"Suffering?" my grandmother laughed. "You call that suffering? Eating a luxurious banquet, wearing silk robes, and having people laugh because she disappears with her betrothed? If she wants to know what suffering is, she should try living in a tent with no servants, the way I did when I was planning for Alexius' glorious reentry to the throne."

"That was a long time ago," said my mother, still with little emotion.

"I did not know that I was allowed to resent the actions of your family for only a limited time." I looked up sharply. Surely those were the words my mother had used when talking about my grandmother in the chapel.

My mother had turned white. But if she too recognized the words, she said nothing about them, but returned to the subject of my disappearance with Constantine.

"She made a mistake, true, but I believe it was done in all innocence. Anna is the least deceitful person in the world."

My grandmother ignored this and said, "My father

would have had me whipped if I had behaved in such a way."

"They were gone but a few minutes," my mother protested. "There was no time for anything to happen."

"Oh, so you saw them go, did you?" said my grandmother. "I am not surprised that you said nothing. You have taught your loose Ducas ways to your daughter."

"*I* have taught her wrongly? Who is the one who teaches her to be cold and cruel? Who tells her to lie, to make promises and not keep them? And who is it that teaches John to repeat what he overhears?"

"I have no idea what you mean," said my grandmother smoothly, and moved as though to leave the room, but my mother rose to her feet and blocked the door.

"Oh, you have no idea what I mean, do you?" she said, her eyes flashing. "How did you know what I said to Alexius in the chapel?"

"Alexius? The chapel?" Grandmother laughed without humor. "You are raving, woman. You Ducases have been known to have weak minds."

"Enough about the Ducases!" shouted my mother, raising her fists as though to strike the older woman. "They were ruling an empire when you were living in a tent and tending goats in your bare feet! We are descended from the great hero Digenis Akritas! Who are you descended from? Barbarians! Illiterate peasants! Even now, you must have your own decrees read aloud to you, because you can't tell an *alpha* from an *omega!*"

Silence fell, but it was a silence that crackled and stung, like the air just before lightning hits. I realized that I had been holding my breath, and made the mistake of audibly releasing it. On hearing me, my grandmother swung around. Her face was contorted, her eyes narrowed.

"This is nonsense," she hissed. "You are not to listen to what that woman says. The Dalassenas and the Comneni are of ancient and noble stock."

"Ancient and noble goatherds!" sneered my mother. But my grandmother ignored her.

"You will behave like a Comnenus," she went on. "You will not see that young man, or any other young man except your brother, unless you have a proper chaperone— and I do *not* mean your mother. You will attend me tomorrow morning in the throne room." She wheeled and made as though to go through the door. But my mother still blocked the exit, and I wondered which one of them would give way. My mother looked my grandmother in the eye—the two women were very much of the same height, although my mother's fair coloring and bright hair made her look somehow taller than the older woman, with her black hair, sallow skin, and dark clothes. They stayed like this for several long seconds, and suddenly my mother smiled coldly.

"You have my permission to withdraw," she said, moving away from the door. And Anna Dalassena swept through, hard shoes clicking on the floor, black skirt swishing on the cloth hanging as my mother let it go.

My mother turned to us, said, "Girls . . ." and fainted.

CHAPTER TWELVE

aria and I were frozen, but fortunately Sophia returned at that moment and caught my mother as she fell. Together she and I put her on the bed, and Maria ran to summon another servant to bring damp cloths and perfumes to help her recover. Mother came to herself in a few minutes, and refusing all offers of help, returned to her own room with her servant supporting her.

I slept poorly that night, and had a disturbing dream. I dreamt that I had walked into the banquet hall, my hand held by Constantine. Both of us wore golden crowns, and we went to take our seats at the heads of the two tables. Suddenly a huge bird, green and gold, but with the face of a human, appeared in front of us, blocking our way. It spoke words that I could not comprehend, but which I could tell had an evil import. I turned in horror to Constantine, but instead of my handsome warrior, I saw that I was holding the paw of a monkey. It laughed and jumped up and down in the way of apes, shouting, "The bird speaks truth! You will never sit in that throne!" and then let go of my hand and whirled away, jumping and leaping on all the banquet tables, upsetting the wine until it flowed like blood over the tablecloths. All around me people were laughing, mouths wide, mockery on their faces, and they all pointed at me as I turned and turned, trying to escape, finding myself ever more hemmed in by crowds that would not let me flee.

I woke up in a sweat, my bedclothes wrapped tight around me. Slowly I unwound them and rose, trying to dispel the evil dream as I made ready for the day. Maria was stirring under her own quilt, and the maids were already laying out our clothes. For me there was a golden-brown robe, one of my better items, but not as formal as that purple-trimmed thing that had caused my father displeasure the day before. We dressed slowly, Maria and I, and we ate the light breakfast that Dora brought for us.

I had no intention of attending my grandmother in the throne room, as she had commanded, but when my father summoned me there before noon, I had no choice but to obey. Sophia gave my hair a hasty dressing, and then accompanied me. When she had seen me safely to the door, she gave my hand a quick squeeze, and left.

Once again I made my approach, and once again I bowed. My heart was pounding, and my head spun, I suppose from the aftereffects of the wine I had drunk the night before. My father bade me rise, and as I did so, I saw that in the throne next to him sat not my mother, but my grandmother. The surprise must have shown on my face, for my father said, "Your mother is unwell this morning, and your grandmother has agreed to assist me today." I nodded, not wanting to say what I was thinking. I was accustomed to seeing my grandmother at my father's side, but I resented her presence in the seat reserved for the empress.

"Come," continued my father. "Come sit on this stool by me and tell of what you have been doing while I have been saving Christendom, little Anna." He gave a self-mocking smile as he said these last words.

"She should be veiled," interrupted my grandmother. "There are other men present."

Indeed, the usual crowd of counselors surrounded the throne platform. My father sighed and motioned to one of his servants, who nodded and left the room, returning in a moment with a plain black veil. My grandmother rose from her throne, and had me turn my back to her and my father as she tied the cords behind my head. As she did so, she leaned forward and whispered in my ear, "Take care how you answer! Our future depends on it!"

Our future? What had her future to do with it? She was an old woman. It was *my* future that concerned me. But I could not answer, for she spun me around to face my father again. He smiled reassuringly and motioned to the stool. I sat on it stiffly, wishing the ordeal were over with.

"Now, tell me, Princess," he began. "How go your studies?"

"Very well, Father," I answered.

"Just 'very well'? What kind of answer is that? Come, daughter, tell me what you like to study and what you do not."

"Indeed, Father, there is nothing I do not like to study," I answered. "Of all subjects, I suppose history and astronomy please me the most."

"And why is that?"

I had never asked myself that question and did not really know the answer. But my grandmother was growing visibly impatient as I hesitated, so I started speaking, hoping the right words would leave my lips.

"I suppose—I suppose—" Then I spoke hastily to avert the storm I saw gathering on Anna Dalassena's face. "I suppose because nothing can change them," I said. "What is past is past, and we can never change history. And the stars are unchanging; they dance each night in the heavens, but one who knows their steps can say what dance they will be doing the next night."

"But all life is change, little Anna," he said. "Why do you dislike change so much?"

Again I did not quite know how to answer, so I said slowly, "Changes are rarely for the better." I did not explain, and hoped he would move on to a different subject rather than ask me for examples of evil change. I could hardly say that the birth of his son had been an unhappy event for me, that I had wanted things to go on the way they always had. His departures for war were changes that upset everyone, and it was only when he returned and life went back to its normal course that we lived happily in the palace. Fortunately, he did not pursue the matter, but went on.

"I understand that you have been learning statecraft with your grandmother," he continued, turning his smile on her. Her thin lips smiled back, but her eyes did not join in as she watched me closely while I nodded agreement.

"And do you learn much from her?" he asked.

I nodded again, hands clenched in my lap. I kept my eyes on him, but wanted so desperately to run away that it was an effort to keep seated.

"She is a good teacher, Anna," he said. "I myself learned much from her, and I would not ever have become emperor if it had not been for her counsel. That is why even now she is my most trusted advisor." This time my grandmother's eyes gleamed as she smiled, turning to look at my father. He returned her gaze for a moment, then turned back to me.

"And what do you learn in your lessons with your grandmother?"

A question I could not answer with a nod. I stumbled through my response, my voice hoarse as though I had a cold. "I learn how wars are waged—how palaces are managed—how treaties are made and broken—how alliances are formed to mutual advantage—"

He held up a hand to stop me. "How treaties are made and *broken*?" His voice slightly emphasized the last word.

"Broken by the other party," my grandmother interrupted smoothly. "And how we must react without dishonor when that happens."

I stared at her, astonished at the bold-faced lie. She had not just talked with me about what to do when the other side failed to live up to its side of the bargain; she had spent long hours detailing how to break a treaty without appearing to do so. But before I could say anything, my father had gone on to another question. "And what have you learned of the history of our family, Anna?" he asked.

I dragged my thoughts away from my grandmother's lie and forced myself to think.

"I have learned little of the Comneni," I answered, "since it seems we did little of note until my great-uncle Isaac became emperor. Previously, we were barons, were we not, and ruled over small holdings that gradually increased through our military might?"

"Indeed so," answered my grandmother. "We have much to be proud of, and it is plain to see that the Ducas blood has not tainted you very deeply." She smiled at me, but instead of feeling proud of the compliment, I suddenly grew enraged at the insult to my mother and to my betrothed. What was there about Ducas blood that would dishonor me, or anyone? And who was she to say *we* have much to proud of? She was not a Comnenus, not even half a Comnenus, as I was.

"One thing Grandmother has not told me much about," I continued, as though I had not heard her, and my father leaned forward, obviously relieved that I was finally speaking of my own volition, "is the history of her own Dalassena family." I turned to my grandmother, and was startled at the venom in her eyes. But I made myself go on, as though I had not noticed, keeping my face expressionless, as I did when playing chess. Don't let your opponent know that her king is in danger, I reminded myself. "There was a Dalassena who married into the Ducases, was there not, Grandmother, a Eudocia Dalassena? Was she a close relation of yours?"

"Hardly," she answered, her face turning dark as she glared at me. "A distant cousin."

"And what," I pursued, "were the Dalassenas doing while the Comneni were increasing their power and the Ducases were consolidating their own?"

My father leaned back and looked at his mother. As she struggled to come up with an answer, he appeared to take pity on her.

"The Dalassenas are an ancient family, too," he replied. "It is through no fault of their own that they were not able to rise to the station that befitted them until—"

"Until they married into it?" I asked, my voice reflecting an innocence that I knew my grandmother would recognize as feigned. Fortunately, my father did not know me so well.

"Indeed," he said, smiling. "And they proved themselves worthy of their new station, and aided it well. You say that your grandmother has told you of her assistance to me in attaining the throne—"

"Oh, she told me that she did more than that, Father," I said in my sweetest voice. I felt myself move across the chessboard until the king was in my sight. "She said that she alone was responsible for your attaining the throne. I assure you, I was fascinated by the tale."

"That is not what I said!" exclaimed my grandmother. "The child has misunderstood me!" A weak attempt to escape checkmate, I thought.

"It would be difficult to misunderstand words like '*I* did it,' Grandmother," I said.

"What are you trying to say?" she asked. I saw her king topple and moved in to capture him.

"Merely that you told me—" but I could not finish the game, for my father raised his hand. He was laughing.

"Enough, enough, ladies! I see that you are two of a kind," he said as we fell silent, glaring at each other. "Neither one of you will admit to being wrong, and neither one of you will change your mind. I see, Mother, that you will have a struggle to maintain your influence if I fall in battle and it is Anna, not I, who sits in this throne!"

I made the sign of the cross to avert the evil omen of his words. My grandmother did not, but regarded me levelly. "Yes," she said finally. "I will indeed." And after making a low, formal bow to my father, she swept from the room without waiting for his permission to withdraw.

CHAPTER THIRTEEN

fter Anna Dalassena left, there was silence in the throne room. I sat frozen to my stool, breathless at the chance I had taken in provoking my grandmother, and giddy with relief that she had not lashed out at me with her tongue. I prayed silently that my father would dismiss me quickly, and he did so after a few moments, murmuring a blessing and kissing me on the forehead. I bowed as quickly as I dared, and entered the corridor, intending to go to my bedchamber. Instead, I felt my arm grasped by a hand. What now? I asked myself wearily, and turned to see who had hold of me. To my relief, it was Simon.

"Little Beetle!" he exclaimed, his ready grin spreading across his round face. "You must see the new additions to the library!" And without waiting for an answer, he bustled off toward that wing of the palace with his characteristic waddle. He didn't wait for me, but if he had been assuming that I would follow, he was right, for I was eager to distract myself with study.

Several open boxes sat on the floor, and Simon bent over one of them, pulling out its contents for me to see. He held a scroll and unrolled it partway to show me the contents. I saw nothing fancy, no illuminations, but beautiful, clear handwriting that filled the page.

"Where did these come from?" I wondered aloud. "Surely it's not booty—the infidels do not write in Greek and Latin."

"In a way, they're booty," Simon said, searching for the perfect place on the shelves to set the scroll he had showed me. "With some of the gold and other treasures your father seized, he ordered that scrolls and books be bought. See—most of them are history."

I bent down in my turn and pulled something out of the wooden box. No scroll, but a bound book, heavy and interesting-looking. It also seemed newer than some of the others. I read the author's name out loud, "Nicephorus Bryennius," and looked up at Simon. "Who is Nicephorus Bryennius?"

"There!" he said with satisfaction, having slid the scroll into what must have been exactly the right spot. "What were you saying?"

"Can't you ever listen to me?" I asked, but Simon was busy examining a new book. "I said, who is Nicephorus Bryennius?"

Simon came over and looked at the book with satisfaction. "This is a real treasure," he said. "Not many of them have been copied yet. It must have cost a pretty penny. The author is a Byzantine, Princess, and a soldier. He knows your father well. He is also a historian, and someday his name will be spoken in the same breath with the names of the greatest historians of the past, like Thucydides and Herodotus."

I examined the book with even more interest. I admired anyone who could unravel the complicated stories of the past and show them in clear form to a reader.

"Someday I too will write history," I said.

Simon chuckled. "More likely to cause history than write it," he said. "Perhaps someday this Bryennius will write a history of the greatest empress that the Byzantine Empire ever knew, Her Imperial Majesty Anna Comnena." He swept a deep bow to me, which I returned to him.

"And of course my chief advisor, Chancellor Simon, will be shown as the great mind and counselor he really is!"

"Unlikely, Little Beetle. Can you imagine your grandmother allowing a slave to advise you along with her?"

"What will she have to say about it? I will be empress, and I will do whatever I want, just as my father does."

"Your father does little without consulting his mother, Princess."

"True," I admitted, sitting down on one of the unopened boxes. "But I won't have to do that. My father is not as strong as I am. He does not see how she manipulates him." I slid my eyes toward Simon to see how he reacted to this treasonous talk, but he made no reaction, so I went on. "I won't have to listen to anyone I don't want to. Anyway, you're a lot more intelligent than that old woman. And I like you much more."

"And what will be your first act as empress?" he inquired, still busily examining and shelving books.

I did not need to think; I had already planned this for years.

"I will exile John," I said. "I will send him to a cold place, like the mountains, and not allow him ever to enter the city again."

"That seems rather harsh, don't you think?"

"It's not as harsh as what I would really like to do. I would like to have him blinded and executed. Did you know that the very day I first saw him I tried to kill him?"

Simon's attention had been drawn back to his new books, and I could see that he was no longer paying attention to me, for he merely murmured and continued in his work. I went on.

"And then, I would make my grandmother fall to her knees in front of me and swear that the Dalassena family is nothing, that the Ducases are far superior to them. And then I would wed Constantine, and I would allow him to be crowned emperor, and we would rule together and undo all the evil that my grandmother has done."

Simon merely grunted again, so I left him to his pleasurable task. I returned to my chamber, bearing Bryennius' book with me, feeling more cheerful than I had since my father's return, and awaited the summons to dinner.

I became absorbed in the book and did not notice how late it had gotten until I realized that it was getting dark, and difficult to read the words on the page. As I made my way to the door to find out why I had not been called to the meal, the hanging swung open, and in burst my grandmother, followed closely by my father, who was clutching John by the hand. The two adults looked furious, but John had such a smug expression that I feared something dreadful was about to happen.

And I was right. My grandmother seized me by the shoulders and shook me until my teeth rattled. "You dare!" she gasped, as though she could not catch her breath. "You dare conspire against me! You dare threaten to kill your brother, the only son of your father?"

Stunned, I looked from her to my father. He was shaking. "Anna, explain yourself immediately!" he said.

"C-C-Conspire?" I stammered. "Kill? What are you talking about?"

My father pushed John forward. "Tell her what you heard," he commanded, "and you, Anna, contradict him if you dare."

"I had been studying alone in the library," he said, and with that last word, my heart sank, and the world turned ashen. I hardly heard the rest of his words as they came glibly off his forked tongue. I wanted to ask how he could have been studying—he who could not even read. But I knew I had to be silent until he finished his story.

John went on, "I had been studying so hard and for so long that I fell asleep behind one of those big boxes that arrived there today. But voices woke me up. Anna was saying that she had already tried to kill me once, and that she was going to do it again. She also called my grandmother evil, and said that the Dalassenas were nothing. She also said——"

"Enough," my father interrupted, fixing me with his dark eyes. "Anna, is this true?"

What could I say? I had never told my father a lie in my life. Feebly, I tried to excuse myself. "Father, when I said I tried to kill John, I didn't mean it, it was the first time I ever saw him, and I was just a child, and I resented the way he took everyone's attention. I never touched him——I have never harmed him, you can ask anybody!"

"I will," my father said grimly. "These are serious charges, Princess. Rest assured that I will find out the truth behind them." He turned back to the door. "Guard!" he said. One of the huge doormen appeared. "Let no one enter or leave this room, except for the Princess Maria and the two maids that attend on the princesses." The guard nodded and withdrew.

I sat on the edge of my bed, utterly defeated. Tears started from my eyes and went down my cheeks in silence, as I refused to allow John and my grandmother the satisfaction of seeing me wipe my face like a child.

There was nothing I could do. But my mother——surely she had some influence on my father. When she spoke to him, all would be well. My mother always made everything well.

"Anna," said my father, bending down now. I dared not look at his face, so kept my own downturned. "If it is true that you were a small child when you threatened your brother, your life will be spared. I will make inquiries tonight and decide what is true and what is not. Your punishment will be considered tomorrow at first light. A guard will come to escort you to the throne room, where you will hear your penalty." And he wheeled from the room, followed by Anna Dalassena, and John, whose face was full of mocking triumph.

I tried to follow them out, but the guard blocked my way.

"Father!" I called down the hall after his retreating back. "Father!" And then in desperation, "Grandmother!" But it was no use; neither one turned around.

The only thing for which I was thankful was that no one had thought to ask me who I had been talking to in the library. I could not tell my father a lie, and I could not refuse to answer him without risking my very life—for he was my emperor before he was my father—but I could never betray Simon, I thought, as my tears turned to sobs.

Now I could only wait for the first light to reveal my fate.

CHAPTER FOURTEEN

hardly slept all night, and when the maids awoke, I rose with them. I knew that my father would already be up and would expect me soon, and I did not like the idea of postponing the ordeal. Sophia dressed me in one of my simplest outfits, and together we awaited the summons. We did not have long to wait, for barely had my untasted breakfast been cleared away before a guard appeared at the door. He had no need to say anything, so I rose, and with Sophia as chaperone, made my way down the familiar corridors to the throne room.

I stayed in my bow so long that I thought my father had forgotten me. But at last, "You may rise," he said. I did so but did not raise my eyes, wishing myself anywhere but there. I stood, swaying a little with fatigue and tension. I wished he would speak, and he finally did.

"I have carefully considered what I have learned," he went on. "I have consulted with my advisors, especially your grandmother. I have also spoken with your brother, although he was reluctant to speak ill of his older sister." I heard a stifled groan from the raised throne area.

Now I did lift my eyes, and saw my mother, looking pale, seated in her throne. Surely she was the one who had reacted with the same disbelief that I felt at hearing of John's "reluctance" to betray me. Her blue eyes, rimmed now with red, looked bleakly at me. There was nothing she could do for me, I knew. My grandmother had been very clever in convincing my father that my mother was just a pretty little thing, good for raising heirs, but without a head for politics. It was too late to change his mind now.

Anna Dalassena was standing in her usual spot at my father's side. Between the thrones stood John, robed in—could it be?—yes, it was a purple robe, made of a design similar to the one that had caused me trouble on my father's return. The sight of him and his little monkey face made me ill, so I looked away from him and up at my father.

He must have slept as little as I had. His face was haggard, and he looked older. His eyes were sad as they gazed at me. Why could I not run to him as I had when he had punished me for misbehaving when I was a little girl? Why could I not sit on his lap and have his strong arms surround me, comforting me, making me know that no matter what I did, I was his daughter, his firstborn, his favorite? But I knew the answer. I was no longer a little girl. And no matter how much he loved me, the empire had to be protected, and if he had been convinced that I was a threat, he would destroy me.

"I have carefully weighed their opinions," he went on. "And I have taken into account that you have devoted yourself to the study of history. You have read in the old chronicles how rulers achieved and kept power by murder, often of their own relatives. We do not do things that way anymore, Anna!" He glared at me. I had no answer to make.

He went on, "I find that as always I agree with your grandmother. She says that you have proven yourself unworthy of the crown." I tried to speak, but he held his hand up to silence me. "I have found that your grandmother is always right about people's characters. She has informed me how you twisted her words in our conversation yesterday, leading me to believe that she would advocate breaking treaties and in other ways deal dishonorably with other nations. Your grandmother would not behave like this, child. I don't know why you wanted me to believe evil of her, and I am disappointed in you." I bowed my head. I could never convince him otherwise; she had covered her tracks too well, and her enemies were silenced by either threats or gold. No one would back me up if I tried to defend myself. I was utterly alone.

My father's next words fell like lead on my ears. "I was wrong to designate you as my heir. You are as of this moment removed from that position."

The room reeled around me, and for an instant I was that little girl again, wanting to cry out at the Venetian ambassadors that it was not true, that *I* was going to inherit, that one day the throne would be mine. A gasp escaped me before I could stop it. But once again I controlled myself, although with even more difficulty than I had at that time. Don't let them see what you're thinking, I said to myself fiercely. A princess does not show on her face what she feels in her heart.

My father's voice reached me as through a fog. "Maria is a dear child, and we all love her, but she is not the sort who can rule. Fortunately..." He paused. "Fortunately, your grandmother has shown me how able John has become in my absence."

My head cleared at these last words. So this was the explanation. Maria was too much a Ducas. My grandmother would never allow someone who so resembled my mother to sit on the high throne. And despite what she said about Ducas weakness and lack of spirit, she knew that Maria had a mind of her own. But little John—ah, he was a different matter. He had managed to hide his domineering nature from her, as he had from my father.

There were other ways in which my grandmother thought she could control John. He could not read, so both would depend on the same scribes to read to them. She would never have to fear that he knew something she did not. He was young and she must think he would be easily formed into the kind of person she thought should rule—ruthless, selfish, with no care for justice. And most of all, he had shown her that he could be led by her will.

That he would be her willing puppet. My mistake, I thought to myself, was that I had let her know that when I was on the throne, I would make up my own mind instead of letting her rule through me, the way she did, I now reluctantly admitted to myself, through my father. Why, I thought, why hadn't I hidden that part of myself? Simon had been right; I shouldn't have flown so near the sun.

"You can't!" Suddenly my mother's voice rang out, making me jump, and she leaped from her throne. "It's all your mother's doing! She has never liked my family and is determined to keep a Ducas off the throne, even a distant cousin like Constantine. I have kept silent at her misdeeds until now, out of respect for my emperor, but this injustice is too much. Anna is your firstborn; she is even named for your mother. She has been expecting the throne all her life. She is more intelligent than that boy will ever be—he can't even read, despite Simon's many attempts to teach him. And Anna is not deceitful and malicious, the way he is!"

"Silence!" I listened as my father spoke in an angrier tone than I ever remembered hearing from him. "Are you mad? That is your own son you belittle. And in any case, you have no say in the matter. The throne is mine to pass on as I think best."

"And what of Constantine?" she demanded, as though she had not heard him. "You agreed long ago that he would sit at Anna's side in the throne room."

This time, my father hesitated before replying. "I will admit that Constantine Ducas is an able man, and he will

117

do well in whatever sphere destiny holds for him," he said "But the throne is not to be his destiny. He will understand. He is my comrade-at-arms, and knows that I must make decisions for the good of the empire, despite personal feelings."

"You gave your word!" said my mother. "If he weren't Ducas, your mother would agree that Constantine is the best man to continue your work. John is still a child; he was raised by servants after I became ill when he was a baby, and learned bad habits from them. Anna was raised to be empress. Even your mother has to acknowledge that Anna is better prepared to rule than—"

"Enough! You have had your say, and I will have mine John will be the next Emperor of Byzantium! It is my decree. The decree of this emperor."

"Emperor!" she sneered. "Who rules here—you or that woman?" She flung her hand in Anna Dalassena's direction. My grandmother stood motionless, not even looking toward the commotion.

My father rose from his throne, and despite his short stature, in his rage he appeared to tower over my mother. "What treason are you speaking?" he thundered. "Are you saying that I am controlled by my mother?"

"What else would you call it?" my mother cried, her lovely face turning red and shiny. "You don't do anything without her approval, you allow her absolute power when you are not present, and you allow her to change your mind about something you promised years and years ago. *This* is what I was afraid of, *this* is what I was trying to tell you. She is deceitful and cruel! The only good that ha come out of this is that she will lose interest in Anna and stop poisoning her soul any more than she already has!"

My father stood as though stunned. My mother lowered her hands, her hair disheveled, her face streaked with tears. Finally, there was silence, which stretched and stretched until the councillors shifted their weight uneasily. Then my father spoke, in a cold tone I had never heard from him before.

"You are mistaken, madam," he said. "My mother is but one of my advisors. The most trusted, I agree, but the wisest as well. Whom should a man trust, if not his mother? But you do not understand this; you are an unnatural mother who does not love her son." My mother started to speak, but stopped as my father lifted his hand to silence her. He went on, "If it had not been for Anna Dalassena's counsel, I would not be seated on this throne, and you would not be seated here next to me. You would be just one of the pretty Ducas princesses and would never know what it was like to have all this." His hand swept around the room as if to show the treasures, the glass, the mosaics.

"Our daughter has spoken treason and murder," he continued, turning his head to look at me with his black eyes blazing. I could not stand their gaze, and lowered my eyes to the floor. "She is still my daughter, and I still love her, and have no wish to banish her or humiliate her in any way, much less have her tortured and executed, as many would expect." He paused and the room once again reeled around me. He spoke again. "She is not evil, merely young and ambitious. I myself was once young and ambitious, and can understand her. But by her actions she has proven herself unworthy of the throne."

He took a step in my direction. "Princess Anna," he said. "You are still an imperial princess, the daughter of the emperor, and the sister of the heir. You will remain in the palace, and continue in your life the way you always have. But do not entertain any hopes of ever inheriting this throne.

"Hear me!" he said in a loud voice. All the councillors bowed low. He looked around the room full of silent and motionless men. "Hear me!" he said again. "I, Alexius Comnenus, Emperor of Byzantium, conqueror of the infidel, protector of Christendom, declare that from this day, the princess Anna Porphyrogenita Comnena is reduced to the same status as her sister, and that my heir will be John Porphyrogenitus Comnenus!"

John moved forward and bowed to the assembly. As he straightened, so did they, and with one voice they cheered the heir, the prince, the one who would next rule them.

And I had to stand there and listen, knowing that my grandmother had orchestrated this scene, that I was powerless, that I would never have what I wanted, and what was rightfully mine.

CHAPTER
FIFTEEN

 remember little of what happened next. I was led back to my room and ordered to pray for forgiveness. I stayed on my knees for hours, praying not for forgiveness but for revenge, for a bloody death to John, and for my own death. I fell into bed exhausted and slept until my mother called me to her chamber the next day. She was pale and shaky, and told me gently what I had already guessed, that I was not to marry Constantine, since it was no longer required that I ally myself with the Ducas family. A suitable match would be made for me with someone whose allegiance was needed by the emperor. I merely nodded, eyes on the floor. What did I care? My life was over.

Later I heard that Constantine, far from being angered when he heard the news of our broken betrothal, fell to his knees and swore eternal allegiance to his new emperor. He had shown his loyalty to my father by this action, and joined him when he left for yet another war.

I joined the rest of the imperial family in the church before my father departed, and we all prayed formally for his safe return. When we gathered in the courtyard to make our farewells, he blessed me as he did Maria and John and my cousins, but his lips felt cold, and his hand barely touched my bowed head.

What solace I found came from my studies. As we imperial children were needing less of his tutoring, Simon took over the duties of the librarian. Even when we both worked in silence, his presence was soothing. Under his guidance, I studied for hours every day, bending over the books, all with different styles of writing, until my eyes glazed and my head swam. But every time I stopped, images of myself on the throne, the golden Constantine next to me, would fill my head. I would force myself to read more until I was so weary that when I finally tumbled into bed, Sophia had to undress my motionless form, and every night I slept a deep, dreamless sleep.

When I was too tired even to read, I would lie on the carpet in the classroom and ask Simon for stories. His voice calmed me, and his tales distracted me. As I reached my thirteenth year, he discouraged this practice as unseemly for a nearly full-grown woman, but sometimes he would still indulge me. Occasionally he would tell me about the old gods, but now that I knew they were dead, as Father Agathos had said, I was less interested in them than in the tales of earlier rulers of our empire.

"Empress Zoë," I would say to him.

"This is not a story for young ears," he would say.

"Empress Zoë," I would repeat.

"Empress Zoë," he would say with a sigh. "She would be about the age of your grandmother, I suppose, if she were still alive. Are you sure you want to hear this yet again, Little Beetle?"

"Empress Zoë," I would say for a third time, and Simon would hurry through the recital of the facts that I so relished hearing.

"She was married to the Emperor Romanus III but was in love with another, Michael the Paphlagonian. She ordered her husband murdered, married Michael, and had him crowned emperor."

He would always stop here, until I prompted him with, "And then?"

"Well, and then Michael died. I don't really know what happened to him, but in a short time his widow was married to her last husband, Constantine IX Monomachus."

I would wait a few minutes to savor the tale. Then, "Irene," I would say.

"Oh, Empress Irene lived hundreds of years ago. She called herself king instead of queen, because she would not admit the power of any man over her. When her son reached legal age to rule, she refused to turn the throne over to him. When he threatened to have her forcibly removed, she had him dragged to the purple bedchamber where she had given birth to him."

"And then?" This was my favorite part of the story, but Simon was always reluctant to tell it.

"Then she had her slaves blind him, in front of her eyes. She shouted to him, loudly enough to make herself heard over his screams, 'The room where you first saw the light shall be the last place you ever see the light!'"

"And he never tried to take the throne again," I would say, satisfied.

"How could he, Little Beetle? He was a broken man."

I found these stories satisfying. I knew my mother did not approve of them, but I also knew that she did not understand the thirst for revenge. So I spent as much time as I could in Simon's company, begging him for more. He finally either ran out of tales or got tired of repeating them, and so gave me histories to read for myself. Psellus' *Chronographia*, with its portraits of fourteen great rulers of our empire, became my obsession. I decided to write a life of my father, taking the *Chronographia* as inspiration. When he came back he would see how much I had learned, and realize my devotion to him. I had given up all hope of regaining the throne, but I still longed for my father to forgive me and love me as he had before.

I was at work on this task in the library one day shortly after my thirteenth birthday when Sophia came into the room. Her face looked even homelier than usual, for I could see that she had been crying. She entered my presence slowly, her lips pressed tight.

"Have you still not learned to bow?" I asked, but more out of habit than anything else. I was resigned to the fact that Sophia would never be a proper servant. But instead of prostrating herself on the floor, she said, "Your Majesty, I have been instructed to tell you some bad news."

I stood up, my hand to my throat, my heart racing. My father was safe with the pope, working out some diplomatic matter—surely nothing could have happened to him in the safety of the papal palace? My mother?

"What is it?" I managed to say.

"It is that your mother's cousin, Constantine Ducas, has died."

Died? The golden Constantine? I clutched the edge of the table for support, scattering pens and paper. Simon, hearing the commotion, moved swiftly to my side, and grasped my arm to keep me from falling.

"Died?" I said when I felt in command of my tongue. "Who murdered him?"

"He was not murdered, Your Majesty," she said. "He fell in battle. They say he died instantly, and felt no pain."

Simon lowered me back to my chair, but I shooed him away. There was a drumming in my ears, and I began to tremble as I absorbed what I had heard.

So Constantine was dead. He had been dead to me for a long time, at least officially. But I had still sometimes caught glimpses of him on the polo ground where we had first met, in the throne room, or in a parade with my father. I knew he was not married—we would all have been summoned to the wedding of a relation—and I still thought that someday my father might see an advantage to my marrying him. I knew that it was a foolish hope, but I had so little to hope for that I clung to it desperately.

I turned back to my books, trying to lose myself in

study. For once I was not successful. I fled to my room, which was mercifully empty. I sobbed and sobbed into my pillow. What crime had I committed that everything was being taken away from me?

I refused to come down to dinner, saying I had a headache. I sat on a chair, staring at the torch, watching the flames flicker whenever anyone passed in the hallway, causing a breeze through the open door. I could see shapes in the flame—first myself as a little girl, seeing John for the first time, then my grandmother, schooling me in the arts I was to need in my glorious future life, then my father, returning battle-stained from war. But mostly I saw Constantine, walking so gracefully he seemed to be dancing, his golden hair shining in the light, his ready smile, the scar on his cheek. In the flames he seemed to move closer to me, then recede, then move closer, finally vanishing altogether as I fell asleep, exhausted.

When I woke up, a hollow feeling had invaded my chest. I sat up in my bed (where someone must have moved me) and looked around. Sophia's place was empty. She has gone to the privy, I thought. The hot, stuffy air of the bedchamber was oppressive, and I suddenly longed for a breath of cool night air. Careful not to disturb Maria, who slumbered next to me, I eased aside the heavy hanging and slipped through the opening, then moved down the hall, my bare feet noiseless on the stone floor.

I had never been alone in the corridor after dark. Its familiar daytime aspect seemed utterly changed without the usual throng of people walking briskly up and down. The stone floor was icy under my feet, and the walls, as I pressed against them, were no warmer. Every few yards a torch flared and flickered, making strange shadows dance on the walls. I passed a few doors, each covered by a thick cloth to keep noises and drafts out, and I tiptoed past the guards' room and up the stairs to the battlements.

Here the moonless sky shone with stars. Simon had taught me how to identify the constellations, and I was grateful that they at least were unchanging, following the pattern that had been ordained for them. Nothing done by humans could alter their destiny. There was Orion, the great hunter, his faithful dog, Sirius, at his heel. The Dragon curled around the sky, and there—

What was that? A sound came from behind a pillar on my left. I had come up so quietly that I hoped that whoever was there didn't know they had company. If I slipped away now, no one would ever know I had left my bed. As I backed away, my feet made a small noise. But it was enough for the person behind the pillar. A shape moved out, and a voice said, "Malik?"

I froze. The form came closer, and in the bright starlight I could see that it was Sophia.

"Malik?" she said again. Then, as I moved out of the shadow, she gasped. Her hand flew to her mouth, and she threw herself on the stones, her head pressed against my foot.

Finally, the proper attitude of submission. I stood there, watching her humiliation, and wondering in the back of my mind why I did not find it satisfying. I sighed, then reached down and pulled her up.

"What are you doing here?" I asked.

"What are *you*?" she responded, then clapped her hand to her mouth, evidently realizing the impertinence of her question. "I—I'm sorry, Princess. Forgive me; I was expecting someone else."

"Who is Malik?" I asked.

She looked away over the battlement without answering. I looked too, and could see now what she had been waiting for. A dark form was moving toward the stairway at the foot of the tower.

"Who is that?" I demanded, pointing at the shape. Still she did not answer, but bit her lip. Tears started from her eyes.

"I could have you both put to death! I *will* have you both put to death! Tell me instantly who that person is, or I will have him executed as a burglar!"

"Oh, no, Princess! He's not a burglar, he's a good man, he's from my village, he's the one I was supposed to marry. He bought his way out of slavery and has been looking for me ever since—"

"Cease your babbling!" I had not heard so many words from her mouth since she had joined our household. "Are you telling me that you are meeting him here by arrangement? Were you planning to run away? The punishment for a slave who runs away is beheading. Were you aware of that?"

"No, Princess, not running away! He comes here every month to tell me how much money he has saved. He's going to buy me out of slavery and then we'll get married. Princess, if you knew him, if you knew what an honorable man he is, you'd know he would never ask me to run away!"

At that moment a shout came from below. Sophia flew to the battlement and let out a scream, quickly stifled when I clamped my hand over her mouth. Down below, we could see a man struggling in the arms of three palace guards. Before I could think what I was doing, I turned and ran down the tower stairs, Sophia close at my heels.

I burst through the door. Two of the guards whirled around, swords drawn. When they saw me, they lowered their weapons, appearing thoroughly confused. They seemed about to speak when the door flew open once again, and out came a little, round shape. My knees grew weak with relief as I recognized Simon.

"What is all this commotion? Are you soldiers brawling again? Don't you know that I need my sleep?" One of the guards indicated me without a word. Simon looked at me, his jaw dropping open.

"Princess—" he began.

"Master Tutor," I interrupted. "Where have you been?" They all joined Simon in staring at me. What could I say? I could see, above Simon's head, the lovely constellation of the Pleiades. This gave me an idea.

"Many of the constellations have set already," I said, "and our night is wasted. It will be a full month before the dark of the moon again, and I was particularly interested in learning astrology right now."

"Princess—" he started again, bewilderment showing on his face.

"Do not interrupt me," I said, desperate for him to stop talking. "You are growing altogether too familiar. I could have you whipped. I *should* have you whipped!" I stamped my foot for emphasis.

That closed his mouth. I had never spoken to Simon that way before. He stared at me in silence.

One of the guards stepped forward. "Your Majesty," he said. I looked up at him. "What about this one?" He jerked his head in the direction of the man still being tightly held by the other two guards.

I had forgotten the man. Sophia clearly had not; I could see her trembling next to me.

"Oh yes," I said. What could I say now? A chill, whether from the cold night air or from fear crept through my whole being. Then words came to me. "Master Tutor," I said, turning back to Simon, "if you had not slept through your appointment you would have been here to welcome your new manservant, the one we discussed this morning." Simon looked at me wordlessly, evidently convinced that I had lost my mind. I continued, gaining confidence with every word. "You told me that you need someone to help you move boxes and reach for books on the higher shelves. Give him a fair trial and report to me in a month."

I turned to the guards. "Release him," I commanded. They dropped his arms.

Everyone remained silent as they waited for my next command. I suddenly became aware of my bare feet, my thin nightdress clinging to my legs. The silent guards stood in their heavy leather and gleaming helmets, and even Sophia and Simon had the dignity of a robe and sandals. Never mind; I was Princess Anna Comnena, and had no need of fine clothes to prove that I was my father's daughter.

First I addressed the guards. "You are dismissed," I said. "Return to your posts." They bowed and melted away, obviously relieved to be gone. Next was Simon. "I will speak to you in the morning," I said. He too bowed and turned back through the doorway.

Sophia was by now holding the man's hand. I moved closer and looked at him. He was short, with the same light-brown skin as Sophia. His black hair curled around his head. Like Constantine, he had a deep scar on one cheek; a relic, I supposed, of the battle my father's soldiers had waged against his village. He was not a handsome man, but was well built and sturdy, standing firmly on his short legs, his free hand clenched into a fist. Malik kept his chin up and stared at me square in the eyes with his black ones. The direct gaze made me uncomfortable, so I turned to Sophia. Her round eyes also stared back at me, the tears drying on her cheeks.

"Take him to the menservants' quarters," I said. "We will speak in the morning." She fell to the ground, embracing my ankles.

"Get up," I said. I was warm from my triumph, and not in the mood to deal with her gratitude. She stood with head lowered, her hand once again in Malik's. "Leave me," I said. They turned to go, but as they reached the door, Sophia looked back at me.

"Why, Princess?" she asked.

I thought for a moment. I didn't really know how to say

it. Finally, "For the chalice," I said. "For taking the chalice from my hand the first day."

A little smile crossed her lips. Then she turned away, and still holding the hand of the man she loved, Sophia quietly disappeared through the doorway.

CHAPTER
SIXTEEN

hen I awoke, it was to bright sun and an empty room. The door-hanging swung open, and Sophia's small form entered, carrying a tray. She said, "Here is your breakfast. I told your mother you were unwell, and she ordered everyone to let you sleep." I sat up and arranged myself on the pillows, pushing the tray aside. Sophia still stood in front of me, her head bowed, her hands clasped in front of her.

"Tell me," I said. "Tell me about your meetings with that man."

"Malik and I grew up together," she said quietly. "Our fathers' lands adjoined each other, and when we were old enough, we were betrothed. He was captured during the battle, and was sold as a slave. He had a kind master who let him keep a portion of what he earned when he was hired out, and he saved every coin. He bought his freedom two years ago, and has been looking for me ever since.

"One day last year, when I was at the market, he finally found me. Oh, Princess—it was like seeing my mother and father again, like seeing my sister and brothers. He spoke in our language; he made me remember all those who died. He told me he had never forgotten me and wanted to buy my freedom. It's hard, but he has managed to save almost half of what he would need. Whenever he can get away, at the dark of the moon, he comes here. We meet for just a few minutes—I'm so afraid of being found out. We talk, I give him any coins that have come my way—that's all, I swear it!"

"And what makes you think you can buy your freedom? I can raise your price to any level I want!"

"I have already spoken to your mother while you slept," she answered, her square jaw set firmly. "She is the one who purchased me, so she knows what is my worth. She has named a fair price for my freedom."

I had grown accustomed to Sophia; I even would have said, if it had not sounded so absurd, that I liked her. I had to find some way to keep her with me.

"How do I know he isn't plotting to overthrow my father?"

"He cares nothing about politics! He was a farmer's son, just as I was a farmer's daughter. Malik has no interest in who leads the empire. Nor do I!"

I found it hard to believe that anyone could be indifferent to the ruling of the empire. But I stood up. "Dress me," I commanded. "I'll have to see for myself."

Sophia ran to pull a robe from the chest at the foot of my bed. As she fastened the dozens of tiny buttons down my back, her fingers felt like ice. She spoke no more, just tied and fastened until I was ready. I hastened out of the room, with Sophia at my heels.

The hall had now returned to its normal daytime appearance, with servants and guards going about their business. I hurried along and pushed aside the heavy hanging covering the library door, expecting to see Simon there. Instead, a tall, stooped man wearing the long robes of a scholar stood with his back to the door, inspecting the books on the tall shelves. He turned at the sound of our entry, then bowed low.

"Your Majesty," he said.

"Where is Simon?" I demanded.

"The librarian?" he asked. "He has gone out with a new servant, I understand. He left me here to examine the books."

"When will he be back?"

"He didn't say, Your Majesty. Is there something I can help you find?"

This amused me, even in my impatience. No one knew this library better than I, especially the history books where the man was standing.

"No," I said. "It is Simon I require. Sophia! Go find Simon," I ordered. "Tell him that I require him and that new servant here instantly."

Sophia hesitated, glancing at the man.

"Never mind that," I whispered. "You can leave me alone with him—there are dozens of guards within earshot. Just hurry!" Sophia left.

The man stood, looking at me, holding an open book. I recognized it as one of my favorites. He saw my glance and handed it to me.

"You know this?" he asked. I ran my eyes over the familiar words.

"Thucydides," I said. "He was a great historian. But Herodotus—"

I suddenly remembered that I was in conversation with a stranger, and fell silent. He didn't appear disturbed by my sudden change, just quietly took the book and returned it to its proper place.

He turned again to face me. "Herodotus?" he prompted.

"The father of history," I said. "Before him people just repeated what they had heard about the past and did not bother to find out the truth."

"And what is the truth?" he questioned, sounding like Pontius Pilate in the Bible.

"The truth—what really happened—what people really did and really said. Not what the gods made them do, but what greed and lust for power made them do."

Before either one of us could speak again, the door flew open and Simon shot in, followed closely by Sophia. As he caught sight of me standing near the stranger, he shot me a warning glance. I understood, and withdrew a few paces, asking him with my eyes if I was now at the proper distance. He nodded, then belatedly bowed low.

"Your Majesty," he said.

"Master Librarian," I answered. "How do you find your new servant?"

I hoped that Malik and Sophia between them had explained the situation to him. "He appears satisfactory," he said. "I only hope that a freedman will not be discontented taking orders from a slave."

I winced at this reminder of my harsh words of the night before. But it was unseemly for a princess to apologize, so I merely cast him what I hoped was a penitent look. After a moment, Simon gave me a little smile. I was forgiven.

"I doubt he will find anything to complain of," I said.

All this time I had forgotten the other man, but Simon now caught sight of him, and bowed hastily.

"My Lord Bryennius," said Simon. "Pray excuse me. May I present to you Her Imperial Highness, the Princess Anna Comnena, firstborn of the emperor?"

Bryennius—this must be the great historian, Nicephorus Bryennius. Simon had said that someday when the great historians were named, Bryennius' name would be on that list. My cheeks burned as I recalled the history lesson I had been giving him. It irked me to see him trying to repress a smile as though he knew what I was thinking.

"I have heard your name, of course," I said. "What is your purpose in visiting our palace? Are you looking for material for a history?"

Now it was the historian's turn to flush. He looked at

Simon as though for assistance, but Simon looked down at the floor. "Did they not tell you, Princess?" he asked.

"Tell me what? Simon, what is he talking about?" If I had not been thirteen years old, I would have stamped my foot the way I used to, when I was in a temper as a child.

"Your father has returned home," Bryennius said. I whirled to Simon and he nodded. The stranger was still talking, and I found it hard to pay attention to him, as I was itching to go find my father. But his next words made me forget everything else. "Your father summoned me to accompany him here," he said. "I am surprised no one has told you. He has commanded me to marry you, Princess Anna."

My father had *commanded* him to marry me? Bryennius must have seen and understood my expression, for he hastily added, "Not that commands are necessary, you understand. I am honored to be told to do that which I would choose freely for myself."

It was fortunate, I thought, that his writing style was superior to his speaking style, otherwise his histories would be tedious to read. Bryennius turned tactfully to Simon and said, "Master Librarian, your works here are indeed as extensive as I had been led to believe. Perhaps you will show me more?" The two of them moved down the aisles, Simon casting an anxious look at me.

Not that he need worry. I knew that I should have to marry soon, and this Bryennius seemed as good a choice as any. I pushed out of my mind the thought of the golden Constantine, galloping after my father on his brown horse. Constantine was dead, just as my hopes for the throne were dead. There was no need even to think of him. So why not a historian? At least we would have something to talk about.

So I guessed why I was wanted when Sophia came to me later that day to tell me that my father required my presence in the throne room.

"That man's with him," she whispered as we hastened down the corridor. "The one who said he was commanded—" she stopped.

"Commanded to marry me," I finished for her. "You can say it, Sophia; I am thirteen years old, and it is time my father found me a husband." She nodded wordlessly, then pulled aside the hanging over the throne-room door, staying out in the corridor as I advanced into the room. Though I modestly lowered my eyes to the floor, I could see a crowd of men around my father and mother on their high thrones.

It was a bright afternoon, and the light slanting through the high windows beat down on the polished floor, making the marble gleam like jewels. As I had so many times, I studied the colors as my feet went over them: red, green, black, white. When the pattern changed, I knew without raising my eyes that I was close to the throne. I stretched out full-length on the floor, my face in my hands.

My father's voice, surprisingly gentle, said, "You may arise, daughter." Usually in public he called me Princess or Your Majesty. The unexpected "daughter" brought tears to my eyes and a hard lump to my chest. I swallowed, trying to push the lump down, and stood, grateful to be standing semiconcealed in the shadow.

"I hear you have spoiled my surprise," my father said. His voice sounded as though he were smiling; I looked up and saw that indeed he was. Emboldened by his warmth, so unexpected after our last meeting in this room, I looked up farther and saw my mother seated in the cedar throne on his left. She looked pale and tired.

I should have lowered my eyes then. If I had, I would not have seen the little monkey, the one they called the prince, standing to my father's right. And not only did he have Constantine's former place of honor—not only was he standing, gazing proudly out at the ministers while I stood with my head humbly and properly bowed, but he was dressed in a miniature copy of my father's imperial suit. He was wearing purple silk, and had a diadem on his head that might, at first glance, be mistaken for a tiny crown. I was suddenly conscious of the rumpled linen robe I had hastily girdled on.

How old was the monkey now—eight? Yes, eight, older than I had been when he was born. I considered that fact with some satisfaction. My parents were still young enough to have more children. You may be the heir now, I thought. But you never know what will happen. Don't forget Fate. And Vengeance.

My father was twisting the gold ring on his finger, a sign that he was not as calm as he appeared. "The choice of your husband is mine and mine alone to make," he went on, looking at my mother, who set her lips tight and turned her head away. Aha, I thought—she doesn't want me to marry this man. She still wants to ally the house of Comnenus with her own Ducas family. Her marriage to my father had formed the alliance; mine with Constantine would have cemented it. Was there another Ducas prince who could wed me? Was that what my mother would prefer?

My father went on, "—but I would never force you, my daughter, to marry against your will. Tell me, is this man satisfactory to you?" He gestured behind him, and Bryennius stepped forward from among the crowd of ministers. I considered the tall man with the stooped shoulders. Although he was older, his beard and hair were untouched by gray. He was a famous historian and so must be intelligent, and he had no obvious physical defects. Anyway, what did it matter? But I was pleased that my father had consulted me before making a final decision.

"Yes," I said. "Yes, he is acceptable."

My father smiled, stood, and stepped down to me. Reaching for my hand, he led me up the steps to the throne and turned us around to face the ranks. I carefully positioned myself so that I stood directly in front of the little boy, blocking him from the crowd. My father apparently did not notice what I had done, for he said in his clear, ringing voice, "We will celebrate the betrothal of my beloved daughter, Princess Anna Porphyrogenita Comnena, to the historian and my comrade-at-arms, Nicephorus Bryennius, with a banquet this evening. You are all commanded to attend."

It was only after I left the room that I realized that a banquet of that importance takes weeks to plan. My consent had been assumed, despite my father's words. But it made little difference to me. I had come to realize that my wishes were not to be granted, that what I wanted and what happened had very little to do with each other. Someday that would change. I was patient. I could wait.

CHAPTER
SEVENTEEN

ere, in the cold convent in the mountains, I often think of that long-ago betrothal feast. No one here cares much for food, and while we eat, there is silence, save for the voice of the lectrix, the nun who reads to us from the Bible. But at my banquet there was rich food of many kinds, and the hall rang with song and laughter and conversation.

The feast was splendid, and, as I had realized, had obviously been planned for weeks. At betrothal feasts the men and the women were allowed to dine together, and shrieks of laughter and loud conversations came from all sides. As the guests of honor, my future husband and I sat between the emperor and the empress, with Anna

Dalassena on my father's other side. John, to my satisfaction, was relegated to a stool farther down the table, with Maria and our numerous cousins.

I lost track of the courses as I sat on my high purple pillow between my father and Nicephorus Bryennius. We had huge roasts of pork, carved into exquisite shapes by my father's experts. We ate fish from both the rivers and the sea, one of them with my favorite green sauce. Fat ducks stuffed with raisins. Boiled chicken. Tiny fried artichokes that you could pop whole into your mouth. Sweet asparagus, many different salads. And fruit: apples, melons, dates.

There were hundreds of guests. Aunts, uncles, cousins, and courtiers—people familiar to me since my childhood—mingled with foreign visitors, and the babble of many tongues was deafening. I looked down the long rows of tables. There was redheaded Maria, soon to be betrothed herself. I caught a glimpse of a head of short gold hair and my heart skipped a beat. Was it Constantine? No, of course it couldn't be. Still, my appetite suddenly deserted me, and I leaned back in my chair, feeling ill. But I knew better, this time, than to leave the room. So I squeezed my eyes shut, trying to keep from crying. A few tears oozed out and flowed down my cheeks as I remembered that long-ago conversation with Constantine. "Our first meeting was sweet," he had said. My first meeting with Bryennius had not been unpleasant, but there had been nothing particularly sweet about it.

No one noticed my silence or my tears in the confusion of the banquet. Servants constantly moved among the tables, pouring red wine into the goblets. The company grew louder and louder, singing bridal songs. Some of them were in such ancient language that I could not comprehend all the words. But I understood enough to make me blush. I thought my mother would be scandalized, but she was singing with the rest of them. Her cheeks were flushed, and she laughed long and loud at some of the songs.

A servant refilled my goblet and I drank thirstily. My appetite made a weak return. The company feasted for hours. Occasionally I glanced over at Nicephorus Bryennius, who ate and drank eagerly. I knew he had recently returned from the war with my father and had probably been on short rations, but still I was scornful that he did not show the restraint one would expect of a scholar.

When the banquet drew to a close, diners leaned back from the table, faces greasy, belts loosened. A few had to be led from the room, as they were overcome by wine and heat. Everyone must have been eager to lie down, and I expected to hear my father dismiss the company, when I saw the priest approaching.

Father Agathos' long robes were rumpled, and his beard seemed to have caught a little of everything he had eaten. My mother stood and motioned Bryennius and me to follow suit. I wished I had managed to slip away, but there was nothing for it now; I had to stay. I knelt on a cushion next to Bryennius and resigned myself to a long wait.

The priest started a prayer. We repeated the responses at the proper time—at least those of us who were not overcome by feasting. Father Agathos finished one prayer, and to my despair started another.

". . . and for the return of His Majesty's servants, and for the destruction of hordes of infidel Turks . . ." Sophia's words came back to me: "I lived with my mother and father and brothers and little sister in a village far from Constantinople." These were some of the infidel Turks Father Agathos was referring to. I pushed the thought from my mind.

Finally the priest reached the end of the blessing, sprinkled us with holy water, and after making a deep bow, withdrew. But escape was still not possible, for now Bryennius rose from his seat. All eyes turned in our direction. Bryennius took from a servant a richly decorated cedar box, its smell reminding me of the throne room. He opened the jeweled lid and pulled out a long belt, made of heavy links of gold, hammered flat and joined in such a way that the belt looked as though it were made of liquid fire. Holding it stretched between his two palms, he turned to me and bowed, saying, "With this girdle I make you my affianced bride," and before I knew what he was doing, he had passed it around my waist and was fastening the clasp. I shrank from his touch, despite my efforts not to.

Next he reached back into the box and pulled out two rings, one encrusted with gems and the other in the shape of a snake biting its own tail. He slipped them on my fingers, his hands warm and dry as they held mine. All eyes were still on us, and I knew everyone expected me to say something. My head swam as I searched for words. Then I saw my grandmother's slanted eyes looking at me, with a glint of what had to be satisfaction. So she thought I would freeze, did she? The thought gave me steel and I turned to face Bryennius.

"My lord," I said. My voice sounded clear and strong, and could be heard through the room. "I, the firstborn of the emperor Alexius Comnenus, carry the blood of Digenis Akritas, the great hero who was ancestor of my mother's Ducas family, and the blood of the Comneni, who have fought to redeem the holy city of Jerusalem from the infidels. The emperor has decreed that our family's blood be further enriched by alliance with a great scholar and soldier. In this, as in all other matters, I obey the will of the emperor. What the emperor has once decreed may not be changed."

My grandmother's expression had altered. Instead of holding a glint of triumph, her eyes were veiled, their heavy lids half-closed as she looked at me appraisingly. I knew she had understood me: The emperor had once decreed that I, not John, should rule. This was the decree that I would not permit to be changed. I wondered if the little monkey had understood as well.

I continued. "Nicephorus Bryennius, I am honored by your gifts. By accepting them, I accept your proposal of marriage, as decreed by His Imperial Majesty, Alexius Comnenus." I bowed to Bryennius, who bowed in return. Together we faced the emperor, and both of us knelt. He bade us rise, and dismissed the company.

The banquet was over.

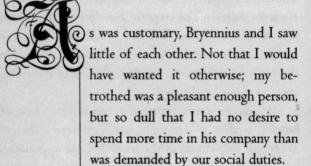

s was customary, Bryennius and I saw little of each other. Not that I would have wanted it otherwise; my betrothed was a pleasant enough person, but so dull that I had no desire to spend more time in his company than was demanded by our social duties.

My father had given me a wing of Balchernae Palace, my favorite of the residences in the imperial compound. I was able to put into practice the household arts I had been learning for several years. After all, I wearily reminded myself as day followed day in tedious sameness, my mother says that a palace is just a large house. I was mistress of the house, and was responsible for all its inhabitants, princess or no.

I had a small consolation when I found that of all the domestic arts I was now called upon to practice, I most enjoyed my skill in medicine. I treated the fevers people came down with in the summer, and children came to me with all their scrapes and bruises for me to anoint.

One afternoon all my tasks had been completed. The servants were sleeping, and I was too restless to lie down. Simon was working in the library, and I wandered through the room, looking for something to read. I pulled a book off the shelf and read the title. To my annoyance, it was a collection of hymns. I was about to find something more suited to my taste, when Simon spoke behind me.

"You might learn something from that book, Little Beetle," he said.

"Why?" I asked, pausing with the book in midair.

"Those are the hymns of Kassia. Do you not remember her?" he asked.

"Kassia?" I remembered the name, but little else. "A little nun who wrote pious verses, was she not?"

"I thought you knew better than to judge without seeing for yourself," he said. "A fine historian you are. Read one and then tell me what you think."

I opened the book at random to a hymn to St. Barbara. I read the opening lines aloud:

"The evil one has been dishonored,
defeated by a woman,
because he held the First-Mother
as an instrument of sin."

Astonishing. This wasn't the usual little nun. Nor was it pious, as I had expected, but a severe condemnation of those who committed wrongs. I turned a few pages and read a poem about Christina the martyr:

"Christina the martyr, holding the cross
in her hand as a mighty weapon,
with faith as a breast plate, hope as a shield,
love as bow, bravely overcame
the punishments of her oppressors,
divinely defeated the evilness of the demons.
Christ provided strength along with your beauty,
that proved unconquerable against both enemies and passions.
It remained firm under the bitter assaults and the most savage
tortures."

I closed the book and held it to my chest. Kassia obviously knew all about injustice, and the importance of remaining strong in the face of your enemy. "I didn't know there were women who wrote like this," I said. "I thought it would all be about forgiveness and accepting your place in the world."

Simon nodded, pleased to have been proved right. "Didn't I ever tell you the story of Kassia and the apple?"

I shook my head and sat down on my usual low stool to listen. I had been missing Simon's stories.

"Kassia," he began, "was a noblewoman. She lived in this city—oh, about four hundred years ago. The custom at that time was for the emperor himself to choose his own bride. All the most beautiful unmarried women would gather in the palace and the emperor would walk among them until he saw the one he wanted. I suppose his advisors would tell him ahead of time which one was the most suitable, so he would not unknowingly choose a woman deficient in morals or in wit, but in any case the choice was his alone.

"In his hand, the emperor carried a golden apple. When he found the woman he was to marry, he would hand it to her. When the emperor of four hundred years ago saw Kassia, he was smitten by her beauty and grace, and handed her the apple. But he wanted to make sure she knew just how small was her importance compared with his, so as he gave it to her, he said, 'Through woman has come all evil,' referring, of course, to the mother of the human race, Eve, whose eating of the apple caused mankind to fall.

"Kassia handed him back the apple, refusing the offer of marriage to a man of such small comprehension and one who obviously did not value womankind. The fact that he was emperor did not sway her. She said to him, 'But also through woman better things began,' speaking about Mary, the mother of Jesus Christ. She left the city and became a nun, founding an abbey and writing hymns to the end of her days."

A satisfactory story, I thought, until the end. Only a fool would choose to live in an abbey when she could have a palace!

CHAPTER NINETEEN

lthough as a woman of thirteen I was freed from regular lessons with Simon, I still spent most of my time in the library. My betrothed continued his own historical studies, and as I learned more about history, we found much to discuss, though I did not seek him out for the delight of his conversation or wit. He was also a warrior, but I found it difficult to imagine him on a horse in his long scholar's robes.

This comfortable situation was not to last, for once again my father was called to war. By now I was used to this. So I felt no worry. Nicephorus Bryennius joined him, and I felt a twinge of relief at the prospect of spending time alone again.

But after their departure, I found

myself with too much time and not enough to do. Absorbing though my readings were, I could not keep at them all day. It occurred to me that since my father was absent, my grandmother must be holding audiences in the throne room again. I wondered how John was faring at her side. I knew that I should stay away, but my curiosity was too strong. So, dressed in my finest robe and with as much jewelry as I felt necessary to indicate my status, I made my way down the familiar corridor.

The door was flanked, as always, by burly guards in full armor. They must be new, I thought, as they did not bow at my approach. Rather, one moved to block the doorway. Surprised, I looked up at his face and saw that far from being a new recruit, this guard was a man known to me. "What are you doing?" I demanded. "Do you not recognize me?"

"You are the betrothed of Nicephorus Bryennius, and sister to the heir," he replied, as though repeating words carefully rehearsed.

I fought to keep from showing the shock I felt. Betrothed of? Sister to? Was I not the Imperial Princess Anna Porphyrogenita Comnena, in my own right?

"Let me by," I said, attempting to push past. But he stood firm, and I could not dislodge him. "Move aside, I say! I will enter!" I tried to squirm around him, but suddenly the other guard joined him and the two of them formed a barrier I could not cross. I cried out as one of them seized my wrist and dragged me from the door.

"You dare!" I gasped. "You dare lay a hand on the

daughter of your emperor, Alexius Comnenus! He will have your head! *I* will have your head!"

"Not likely," said a thin voice from the doorway. There stood two figures, both robed in silk, both crowned. The smaller one, who had spoken, was my brother; the larger, my grandmother. Anna Dalassena wore a gleeful smile, and her wrinkled hand grasped the boy's shoulder.

"You forgot your bow to the heir," she said.

My head whirled and my stomach churned, and I suddenly felt I was going to vomit. I fought it back, fiercely forbidding myself to show any weakness. A bow was what they wanted, and a bow was what they would get—but I would face an executioner before I would prostrate myself full-length on the floor. It is proper for a sister to nod to her brother, so this is what I did.

"I hope I find you in health, Little Brother." If they had forbidden the guards to address me by my title, no power on earth could make me call the monkey Your Majesty.

He looked at our grandmother, evidently confused. Good, I said to myself. You thought I would refuse. I know how to play chess, too, Grandmother. Only you would do well to plan your moves further in advance and expect the unexpected. And even though you've found someone to be your puppet, don't count on this half-wit to make any moves without your help.

Before he had a chance to regain his composure, I asked, "What is the meaning of this? At whose orders will the guard not let me pass? Yours?" I addressed my grandmother.

"No, mine," said John.

"Yours? By what right—"

"By right of proclamation," replied my grandmother. "Your father, as always, has decreed that while he is away at war I am to decide all matters as though I were emperor. I have decided that the heir to the throne must start to learn his duties now. It is up to him who attends audiences, and he has decreed that you are not permitted in the throne room. You may return to your books."

Without doubt, I was in check. But it was not checkmate. Surely, surely, my father would return soon—he had said that this latest trip was merely a short campaign to quell unrest along the borders. When he came back he would make all right again.

But this time he was gone two long years. And when he finally came home, I was not permitted to present my case to him, for he returned ill, borne on a litter by four slaves, and for days lay near death in the Pearl Palace, attended constantly by my mother and grandmother. I wanted to help, but my grandmother would not let me in the sickroom.

It was a long, weary time. Anna Dalassena retained power, since my father was too ill to hold audiences or even see petitioners, and his decree making her regent while he was away was held to be in force until he could regain his strength. I was still barred from the throne room, and was too distracted to spend long hours at my books. Simon was too busy for stories and would send me away. I was left with no one but Sophia.

Sophia usually accompanied me to the library. I was under no illusion that she came for the joy of my company.

I knew that she hoped to catch a glimpse of Malik, whom she rarely saw. At these times, I would pretend not to see them when they exchanged smiles, or even touched hands when they thought I was not looking. But he usually would be called upon to move a box, reach a book on a high shelf, or travel into the city to pick up something that Simon had ordered, and Sophia would join me at my worktable.

She, of course, could not read, but she would turn over the pages of the books and look at the pictures while I studied. One of her favorites was a psalm-book my father had had a Frankish monastery create for my mother. I could understand my maid's fascination with the book. The letters were more beautifully formed than I had seen in any other work. Most marvelous of all, every page was illustrated with paintings of angels, shepherds, mountains, blue skies, castles.

I looked over to see what page held her interest so long. She was gazing at a scene richly illustrated with an angel, golden wings spread wide, hovering over a city. Even though the whole picture was no larger than my hand, I could see the town walls, and towers, and even tiny windows in the buildings. In the field outside the city, small people in clothes of many colors were bent over the ground.

"What are they doing, Sophia?" I asked.

"Those are farmers. They're planting crops," she answered.

I looked closer. So that was what the farmers who came to plead with my grandmother were talking about. I had seen gardeners growing flowers and ornamental shrubbery, but had never seen "crops." In the picture I didn't see anything I recognized as food. Then I noticed that some of the figures wore long dresses.

"How odd! There are women outside, in front of men, with no veils on their faces!"

"Most women wear no veils, Your Majesty. It is only in the palace and among the nobility that women must cover their faces."

This was a strange thought. I had never been outside the walls of the city, and rarely outside the palace, except when we moved to the Daphne Palace in summer and back to Balchernae in the winter. And in the palace, a woman would just as soon appear in public without her clothes on as without a veil covering her face.

"This is Constantinople," Sophia said. She went on, "See—here's Balchernae Palace, with your bedroom window that faces the ocean. There's the Daphne Palace, and the church of St. Sophia, and the horse field. And you can see all the other buildings inside the compound."

I bent closer, looking for a picture of myself. But I could not see any figures inside the walls. Hovering directly over the palace was an especially beautiful angel, long wings gleaming with what had to be real gold. This angel's arms were spread wide over the city. I said, an edge of contempt creeping into my voice, "And I suppose my mother would say that this is the guardian angel who is always over the city, looking after us and taking care of us."

Sophia looked surprised. "Of course. Don't you believe in angels, Princess?"

"I am a historian. I believe in what I can see," I said. "I

have never seen an angel, nor have I read of any in my histories. And if there are guardian angels, why do they allow evil to happen? I should think that you, of all people, would know that."

Sophia flushed. "I have had doubts," she said, "but I know that someone is helping me. How else could Malik have found me?"

"Why would he have had to look for you if your village had not been destroyed?" I countered. "Where was your angel when your little sister was killed or enslaved? Where was mine when my grandmother convinced my father to name John his heir?"

Sophia set her jaw stubbornly. "I don't know the answer to that," she said, "and I hope you don't let Father Agathos hear you say such things. I am not a Christian, but he says many wise things, and your mother thinks that everything he says is true. Surely you don't doubt your own mother?"

I did not like being interrogated by a slave, so I turned back to my book.

That night I slept fitfully. I woke up with a start in the darkness. What had I heard? Could it have been the rustle of angel wings overhead? I sat up, careful not to disturb Sophia, who was sleeping on a pallet at the foot of my bed. I listened again. Nothing. But I wanted to be sure, so I slipped out of my bed and stole to the door. Holding my breath, I carefully pushed aside the heavy hanging and slipped through the opening. I moved down the hall, my bare feet almost noiseless on the stone floor. The last time I had been in the corridor alone had been the night Malik had come to the palace. But I was older now, and moved with less fear. Still, I was careful not to be discovered. I had no idea what would be my brother's reaction to this nighttime excursion.

I soon found myself outside on the high battlements. A breeze stirred the air and cooled my moist cheeks. Keeping close to the wall, I craned my neck backward, scanning the sky. There was nothing. The calm stars and the moon shone steadily, with no hovering angel to block them from view. I stayed as long as I dared, slipping behind stone battlements every time I heard a guard go by. Finally, shivering with cold and disappointment, I retraced my steps.

As I lay awake for the rest of the night, I wondered why the psalm-book had pictured something that did not exist, and why my mother spoke of our guardian angel. All I could think was that everyone had lied, and that no one was watching over me.

CHAPTER TWENTY

y father's health was much improved. When the news reached me in the library, I jumped up, uncaring of the self-restraint due my position, and clapped my hands. At last my father would be back, sharing meals with the family, exercising his horses, ruling from his high throne.

But I would have to wait. The emperor was weak, and required a great deal of rest before resuming his duties. As for soldiering, it was doubtful that he would ever go on another campaign. Aside from this latest illness, he had long been troubled with gout and arthritis, making riding on horseback excruciatingly painful. And while earlier rulers had been carried to battle in a litter and observed the action from afar, my father had been a soldier for years before being proclaimed emperor, and I knew that he would never consent to such a humiliation.

It was a joyous afternoon when the emperor's family was allowed to visit him. I was ushered into the sickroom, which was dark, with windows closed to keep off the injurious aspects of the outside air. The room smelled like illness, and like medicine, and it took a few minutes for my breathing to adjust to the close air, and for my eyes to adjust to the darkness. When I could finally see, my heart sank at the sight of my grandmother sitting at the head of my father's bed, John standing at her side, as always.

I knelt by the bed, and felt my father's hand on my head in blessing. I did not trust myself to raise my face, which I knew was shining with tears. Sophia, who had followed me closely, knelt by my side, and surreptitiously pressed a handkerchief into my hand. Taking advantage of the darkness and glad that the high bed partly hid me, I quickly wiped my eyes and passed the handkerchief back to her, then awaited my father's words.

His voice was weak. "I am glad to see you, my daughter," he said. "Are you impatient for the return of your betrothed?"

I raised my head and looked at him. He was thin and his skin looked yellow. I could see that under the blanket his legs and feet were terribly swollen. I was spared the necessity of answering (for what could I say, that I hardly noticed Nicephorus Bryennius' absence?) by my grandmother, who said, "The princess finds consolation for her solitary state in the study of history."

"My scholar," said my father fondly. He started to raise himself up on his pillows but was seized with a fit of coughing. The physician and his assistant hastened to the bedside, and while the physician held my father upright, the younger man poured red wine from a beaker into a small cup, and then carefully poured into it a drop of liquid from a small flask. The physician took the cup and said impatiently, "No, no! That is far too much! Do you want to kill His Majesty?" He poured half the medicated wine into another cup and filled it with more wine, thus diluting the medicine by half. He went back to holding my father up while the assistant helped him drink.

"What are you giving him?" I asked.

"It is a medicine against the cough," he answered curtly. As if I couldn't have deduced that for myself! But if he didn't want to tell me the name of the drug, there was nothing I could do about it. Physicians are notoriously jealous of their knowledge.

Everyone was occupied with my father. Before I knew what I was doing, my hand had flashed out and seized the flask of medicine. No one saw my impulsive action, as it was dark and there was so much confusion brought about by my father's desperate attempts to breathe. All eyes were on the bed. All but Sophia's.

My father finally stopped coughing and lay back on his pillows. Gently my mother wiped a thin stream of spittle from his beard and laid a cloth on his forehead. She said, "You must leave now; His Majesty needs rest. You may give him one kiss before you go."

I panicked. How to explain the flask in my hand? But

before I could drop it, Sophia's strong fingers removed it. I felt dizzy, as though time had reversed its course and I was once more a little girl in the hot courtyard, and Sophia was taking the chalice from me. Saving me. With an effort, I acted as though nothing had happened, and bent to kiss my father on his cheek. I bowed to my mother (ignoring my brother and grandmother as I did so) and led Sophia out of the room.

We said nothing until we were back in my chamber. I made sure the door-hanging was spread tightly across the opening, and then pulled Sophia as far into the room as I could.

"Why did you take that?" I asked.

"Why did *you*?" she retorted. I was too upset to object to her insolence. In any case, I didn't know what to answer. I had seized the flask on an impulse.

"I thought it might be useful," I said.

"Useful in what way?"

I sat down on a stool, suddenly weary of everything; weary of what my life had become, weary of waiting for my father to recover and rescue me from my humiliation, weary of having no say over my own destiny, and suddenly weary of the endless books and stories that seemed more real to me than my life.

"I don't know," I said. "The physician said it was deadly. When my brother becomes emperor I don't want to have to put up with what he and my grandmother do. I don't want to be forced to live the life they make for me. If I have a way out—"

"No!" Sophia said. "You can't do that. If you do, he'll

win! Don't you see? That's what he wants. That's what *she* wants." Sophia was right. I sat on the stool and sobbed, my face down on my knees. Sophia knew me well enough not to try to console me, but fetched me a glass of water when I had ceased.

"You must rest now," she said. "But what of this?" She indicated the flask in her pocket. "May I dispose of it?"

"No," I said. "I may need it." Before she could protest, I added, "And don't leave it in here. My room could be searched at any time. You must take it away."

"Where?" she asked.

I thought for a moment. "Simon," I said. "Give it to Simon, and tell him to keep it for me."

She seemed about to speak, but the habit of obedience was strong now. Still I did not trust her as I watched her move to the door.

"Sophia!" She turned.

"You must swear to deliver it to him, and you must make him swear to keep it for me."

"I can't—"

"Swear!" I said. "Swear, or I will have Malik sent away to the border country, and you will never see him again!"

She winced, and with her eyes downcast, she said, "I swear," and left me.

I must have fallen asleep, for when I awoke a tray of food was on the table next to me. Bread, figs, my favorite fried artichokes—but I was not hungry and pushed the tray away. I drank only the wine. When Sophia came in, she asked, "Was the food not to Your Majesty's liking?"

I shrugged. What did food matter?

This feeling did not change. I could hardly eat, and what I ate I nearly always vomited back up. I did not care, but my mother was concerned. One day she came to the library, where weakness had overtaken me and I had laid my head down on the table in front of me.

"What ails you, daughter?" she asked, smoothing my hair back off my cheek. Her light touch was so soothing that I nearly fell asleep. Instead, I made an effort and sat up, although my head swam.

"Nothing, Mother," I said. "I just don't have much appetite. It must be the hot weather."

"It has been cool for weeks," she replied. "You are thin, Anna. You look like one of the saints in the mosaic in the church, with your huge eyes and thin body."

"At least there's *something* saintly about me," I said, trying to make her smile. But her expression remained serious.

"Don't say that, Anna," she said. "There is much of good in you. You are honest, and honorable. You would never harm a friend, and you have a passion for the truth. I just wish you could be more forgiving."

I knew she was referring to John and my grandmother. I turned my head away, knowing I could not control the loathing on my face but not wanting her to see it. "And have *you* forgiven, Mother?" I asked softly, knowing the impertinence of the question.

She did not reply for so long that I thought she had not heard me, but finally she said, "Daily I pray for the strength to forgive. I find it difficult, but I am trying."

I looked down. I did not want to forgive. I wanted to

continue hating. But I could never admit this to my gentle mother.

"And why do you spend all your days in here?" she asked. "Your sister and cousins are so busy all day, with music and talk, and the children. You hardly see Maria anymore. She notices this and is hurt."

Music and talk did not interest me—and children, I did not have. "I'm sorry," I mumbled. "I'll try to take the time to see her. I don't want to hurt Maria, Mother. Truly I don't. It's just that what I read here is so much more real to me than what goes on in the palace."

"Don't let books take the place of your life," she said, rising. "What happened in the past is dead, and over. There is no way to change the past. You can change only the present."

"Can I, Mother? I don't think so."

She kissed me. "If you can't change it, you can find what is good about it. You are betrothed to a decent, honorable man. You will someday have children of your own. Don't poison them with your hatred. Our Lord says to forgive." She stood, stroked my face again, and said, "Try to eat something." And she withdrew from the room.

Simon had moved into the shadows when my mother started talking, but now he came forward.

"What do you think, Simon?" I asked. "Should I forgive?"

As usual, he answered with a story. "Do you remember the tale of King Thyestes? He stole the throne of Mycenae from his brother, Atreus, by a trick, and then committed adultery with Atreus' wife. Atreus pretended

166

forgiveness and invited Thyestes to a banquet. After Thyestes had dined richly on a stew, Atreus revealed to him that he had eaten his own children."

I shuddered, revolted at the idea of such a banquet. But something in me also understood Atreus' impulse. "But surely Atreus was right not to forgive Thyestes. True, his vengeance was extreme, but Thyestes had stolen his throne and his wife—"

"Thyestes never forgave Atreus for the murder of his children, either," Simon went on, as though he had not heard me. "He laid a curse on the house of Atreus, and in consequence, Atreus' son, Agamemnon, sacrificed his own daughter, Iphigenia, to get a favorable wind to sail to Troy. Agamemnon was in turn murdered by his wife, Clytemnestra, who could not forgive him for the death of her daughter. You see, Little Beetle? Once it starts, it doesn't stop."

I pictured the long chain of kings, starting with Atreus and going on and on and on. I wondered whether Atreus was one of my ancestors. That would explain why I was cursed. But if I was a descendant of Atreus, my brother was too, and if there was any way I could make the curse fall on his head, I determined to do it.

CHAPTER
TWENTY-ONE

My father never returned to his throne. Instead, after appearing to recover for a few weeks, he suddenly relapsed. When they told my mother, her wail could be heard as far away as my apartments. Even now, years later, I can hardly bear to remember my own despair when I learned this news. My father had often been absent, but he had been affectionate to me when I was a little girl. When I was small I had thought of him as the soul of justice. I hoped desperately that he still was, and that if I could just see him, talk to him, I could tell him what had happened, that my grandmother had turned against me when she realized that I would not be her puppet, and that John had fallen under her spell.

If he only knew this, he would surely right this wrong. He had changed his mind before, hadn't he? When Anna Dalassena had not wanted him to have my mother crowned, he had at first gone along with her, and then defied her, hadn't he? Surely he would do the same for me, for his firstborn. But if he died, who could right the wrongs done me?

I spent long hours in the library, and one day was gathering up my papers to leave when John and our grandmother entered. John stood in a shaft of light, dust motes swirling around him. He blinked in the harsh light, and looked down the long rows of books. Our grandmother stood behind him, watching me with her narrow eyes. I stood at my desk, hands on my papers.

"So this is where you spend your days," my brother said. "What is it you're writing?"

On an impulse, I gathered up the papers and thrust them at him. "See for yourself," I snapped. He looked at them, and I could tell by his blank expression that he still could not read. Just as I had thought. He passed the papers to our grandmother, who made an annoyed sound with her tongue, and then said impatiently, "What is this?"

"Why don't you read it for yourself, Grandmother?" I asked, knowing full well that she could not.

"Because I told you to tell me what it is!" she said, stamping her foot impatiently.

"It is a book I am writing," I answered. "The title is *Alexiad*."

"*Alexiad?*" she asked. "What's that?"

"You have heard, Grandmother, of the *Aeneid*, the story of the life of the Roman hero Aeneas? And the *Iliad*, about the city of Ilias?"

"Yes, child, of course I have. Am I to understand that this is a book about Alexius?"

"It is a history," I said. "It tells of the emperor's great deeds: his battles, his war in Jerusalem, his great acts as leader of his people. I want future generations to remember my father."

"*Your* father?" John laughed, a sneering, unpleasant kind of laugh. "What makes you think he is your father?"

What on earth was the little monkey talking about? Bewildered, I made no answer, but John had not waited, in any case. He went on, "You were born after he had been on campaign for many months. I have long suspected that you were not his daughter."

I came from behind my desk, sputtering. "You dare! You dare!" I shouted. "I resemble him even more than you do—everyone says so! And he was gone only six months before my birth, and he returned before I was born and made no attempt to prevent our mother from bringing me into the world in the purple chamber. And what are you saying about our mother? Don't you know what you're calling her when you claim I am not my father's daughter?"

John had backed away from my fury and was now pressed into our grandmother's side, clutching her skirts, his hand to his mouth. He looked three years old, instead of the ten that he now was. With a great effort I stopped shouting, and stood trembling, my fists clenched by my side. John looked up at our grandmother for assistance. She said venomously, "Your mother is a Ducas. Everyone knows what the Ducas women are—pretty, weak fools. I am not saying that what happened was all her fault; your father was often away for long periods and she—"

Before I knew what I was doing, I had flown at the old woman and seized her hair in both hands. I pulled as hard as I could and to my astonishment the black tresses came off in my hands. So all those intricate coils were false, just like her own lying self. She threw her hands to her now bald head and screeched, "You are no princess! And a commoner who strikes a member of the imperial family is put to death—I will spare you this time, but never again, girl!"

She wheeled and fled the room, leaving John defenseless. But he need not have worried; I was not going to touch him. I sat down on a box, my head whirling, trying to grasp what had been said. But John was not finished.

"You may not write your lies about my father," he said. "You must cease from this moment to write your book. You may not cross the threshold of this library again. You, there!" He was addressing Malik. "Sweep up all this rubbish and burn it!" He tossed my papers to the desktop. He stepped to the door and called out. "Guard!" The man appeared and bowed. "Keep this woman from entering the library again," he commanded. "If she tries to come in, throw her in the dungeon and report to me immediately." The guard nodded, and then I left my one refuge—for the last time, as it turned out.

Fleeing to my bedchamber, I paced for hours. What was

John up to now? I could read his mind—or rather my grandmother's—enough to realize that this was probably the first step toward having me removed from the palace altogether. Or were they planning to have me executed? My blood ran cold.

In the meantime, I was banned from the one place where I found solace. If I couldn't use the library, if I couldn't forget the ills done me by the study of the past, how could I bear it? Bitterly I regretted having sent that flask to Simon. I needed it to end my misery. I finally crawled into my bed.

I had not been asleep many hours when a hand seized my shoulder and shook me roughly. I shot up, wide awake, expecting to see a grim-faced soldier who would carry out some further evil scheme of my grandmother's. Instead, I saw Maria bending over me, tears streaming down her face.

"You must make haste, sister!" she sobbed. "It's our father—Mother says he's dying!"

I leaped from my bed and pulled my gown on and, barefoot, flew down the corridor after the disappearing form of my younger sister. We ran out of the palace, across the courtyard, and into my father's palace, where guards were standing at the door. To my relief, they moved aside to let me pass, and I hastened into my father's chamber.

My mother was leaning over the bed, where Maria joined her. Anna Dalassena stood at my father's pillow. Her face was desolate. At last, I thought, she has met something she cannot change. Father Agathos was at the foot of the bed, intoning prayers. My mother implored my father to take some medicine, but he shook his head back and forth on the pillow, whether in refusal or out of pain, I do not know. Maria was silent, staring at him. My father's eyes turned in my direction as I knelt at his side, but there was no trace of his usual welcoming smile. Instead, he muttered something that I could not understand.

"What did you say, Father?" I asked, and bent low over him. But he did not repeat his words, merely started his head-shaking over again, and moaned. I wrung out a cloth in the basin next to his bed and laid it on his forehead, but he soon shook it off. He did not look like an emperor, but rather like any old, sick man.

"Alexius! You must listen to me," my mother said. The motion of his head ceased, and he fixed her with a glassy stare.

"Husband!" she tried again. "What of the succession? Will you not repent of your foolishness and name Anna your successor, as you first promised?"

He moaned again, and shook his head vehemently. Even I had to admit that this was a denial and not a movement of pain. His mother turned on mine and seized her arm. "No more!" she spat. "The succession is determined!" She flung my mother from the bed.

Becoming more agitated, my father clawed with his left hand at his right, where the imperial ring had been since before I was born. He forced out a name. "John," he said, and from the shadows stepped my brother.

"Yes, Your Majesty, I'm here," he said. "What is your will?"

"John," he repeated, and finally managed to pull the heavy gold ring from his finger. He thrust it into the boy's hand, and before anyone could say or do anything, John had seized it and disappeared from the room.

I sprang to my feet to follow him, but guards barred the way. Defeated, I turned back to where my father was lying still now, his breathing labored, sweat pouring down his face. I had loved him more than I had loved anyone else, even Constantine, and he had failed me. He had had the chance to right his wrong, and had not done it. All was over. I did not blame him, but I could not forgive him either.

My mother was crying, huddled on the floor. "Mother—there's nothing we can do about John," I said. "Let us ease my father's way out of this world while we can."

"Do what you like," she said in a flat voice. So for an hour I moistened my father's brow with wet cloths, wiped the sweat from his face, tried to help him drink some wine. But of a sudden his breath stopped, and we knew he was dead.

My mother let out a harsh cry, almost inhuman in its despair. She leaped to her feet, seized a knife, and before anyone could stop her she had hacked off her long red hair, throwing it on the floor. She kicked off her slippers of imperial purple, and with her fingernails tore at her silken gown. Maria and I watched helplessly, afraid to approach her, but Father Agathos seized her hands and held them still, speaking soothingly into her face.

"Daughter—daughter—" he said. "You will see him in Heaven. All will be made new then."

"What care I for Heaven?" she spat in his face. My sister and I gasped; never would I have imagined that our pious mother would speak thus, even in her despair. "What good will Heaven do if this Earth is Hell?"

I agreed with her silently. But I could not give way to hopelessness, as she had; I knew that there was much to do. Even now the maids were closing in on the bed, linen cloths in their hands. My grandmother had withdrawn into a corner, her face white and rigid. My mother and I moved back out of the way of the maids, my mother reluctantly, still sobbing, and held by the priest. We watched as the women stripped the soiled garments off my father and cleansed his body with fragrant water, and then dressed him for the last time in his imperial robes, with his ornate crown and purple slippers. In silence we stood as his body, seeming suddenly shrunken, was carried out of the sickroom by two young priests. Father Agathos followed, repeating the ancient formula, "Depart, Emperor: The King of Kings, Lord of Lords calls you."

My mother, weeping hard now, leaned on me as we followed the procession to the Hall of the Nineteen Couches, where for centuries the body of the emperor has lain in state before burial. I felt my grandmother try to push past us, but I blocked her. Here, at least, the widow must take precedence, even over the mother. John, I suddenly realized, was not there. Everything had happened so fast that I had hardly had time to wonder where he had fled to. Later we found out that he had run to the church of St. Sophia, where he had been crowned emperor in a hasty ceremony.

The following days are a blur in my memory. We had to postpone the funeral until dignitaries and ambassadors from many lands could arrive. Each morning I rose from my bed and attended services, Masses for the repose of my father's soul. I resisted the idea that he needed any intercession to enter Heaven, but participated as was expected of me. I had no need to upset my mother further or to anger my brother. I know that several nights I awoke, screaming with nightmares, to find Sophia's soothing arms around me, her quiet voice hushing me back to sleep.

The day of the funeral was appropriately dreary. Rain fell in torrents, and a wind whipped the procession. My brother led the long funeral train, accompanied by our mother, who looked dazed. Nicephorus Bryennius had hastened home and was at my side, although I hardly noticed his presence. After the services, long and incomprehensible, we were to return to our chambers and rest until the funeral feast, the last of the ceremonies we had to perform.

I was alone in my chamber, for Maria was taking her turn keeping vigil over my father's body in the chapel. Sophia and Dora, along with all the other slaves, were helping prepare for the funeral feast. As I lay on my bed, I heard a stealthy sound at the door. My heart pounding, I waited to see who was coming in.

It was my mother, although I hardly recognized her. Her dress was disheveled, her short hair in disorder around her lovely face, her blue eyes dim with weeping and circled with red. She crept up to my bed, and said, "Oh, Anna, you're awake." I sat up.

"Mother—" I started.

"Hush!" she whispered. Her swollen eyes stared wildly around the room. "We don't have much time."

"Time for what?" I asked, but she clapped her hand over my mouth.

"Don't let anyone hear you!" she whispered. "Do you know what he is calling me?" I did not need to ask "Who?" for it could only be John. I shook my head. "He is calling me an adulteress. He says that your father never wanted to marry me, that he was forced into it. He reminded me that when Alexius was crowned emperor he refused to have me named empress, and when I told him that that was all the doing of that demon, that witch, that Anna Dalassena—oh, forgive me that I ever consented to give you her name!" She stopped talking, and impatiently dashed away the tears that had sprung from her eyes. I was too terrified to say anything, and waited until she had composed herself and started speaking again.

"He is not my son," she whispered vehemently. "No son could say such things about a mother. A devil slipped into my son's cradle when he was a baby and took his place. And we cannot allow him to continue saying these things."

"But, Mother," I said, "how can we stop him?"

She turned her eyes on me, and I could see that they had changed. They were flat and lifeless, and had lost their light, and I shuddered.

"He must die," she said.

CHAPTER
TWENTY-TWO

ie?" I whispered.

"He must be struck down at the funeral banquet," she went on, as though she hadn't heard me. "That way everyone will know that he took the throne wrongfully, and that it is not God's will that he rule. I will do it myself—this hand will strike him down with a dagger as he feasts on what should be yours." She raised her trembling right hand in the air, fingers curled as though clutching a knife.

I crept to the door and looked out, to make sure that no one was listening. The corridor was empty, save for guards standing at the far end.

"You can't," I said, turning to face my mother. "You will be executed—probably blinded and tortured first."

"I don't care," she said. "There is no reason for me to live. The witch and her familiar will torture me anyway, just by being alive and ruling the empire that should be yours and mine."

Silently, I agreed with her. The mere presence of John on the throne, doing everything Anna Dalassena told him, would be intolerable. Only by John's death would life be made bearable again. I pictured myself on the throne, the gold ring on my finger, the crown on my head. I pictured my grandmother prostrate at my feet, begging for mercy—which I would refuse to grant. I saw my mother restored to her high place at banquets. . . .

But if she were caught and executed, I would take no joy in my rule. I looked at her thoughtfully. She was trembling, and her hands were roaming shakily through her hair, as though looking for the tresses she had flung on the floor in my father's death room. I made a decision.

"No, Mother," I said. "I will do it."

She clutched me eagerly. "You will? You could? How will you do it?"

"Never mind," I said. "But I will take care not to be found out. Now, return to your room before anyone comes in and accuses us of conspiracy." Rightly accuses us, I thought. She nodded. Her lips, as they pressed on my forehead, were hard and cold.

I knew what I had to do.

Even as I thought this, Sophia entered the room. She looked exhausted. But I took no pity on her.

"Find Simon," I said. "Find Simon immediately, and tell him he must come here. After you have delivered this message, find me a dress such as the kitchen-women wear." Obedience was by now such a habit with her that she had already started for the door without questioning me. "And Sophia . . ." She turned. "Tell Simon he must bring the flask. You know which flask I mean." She hesitated and seemed about to say something, but instead went out the door.

I paced up and down, waiting impatiently. I had no clear plan in mind, but one was starting to form.

After what seemed an eternity, Simon appeared. He put his bald head in at the door and looked around, obviously uncomfortable at the thought of entering my bedchamber. I seized his arm and dragged him in.

"Did you bring it?" I whispered, after making sure that there was no one in earshot. He nodded, pulling the flask from his sleeve.

"Give it to me!" I commanded, grabbing at his hand. But he evaded my grasp.

"What do you want it for?" he asked.

"I do not have to explain my actions to you, slave!" I said, and saw him wince as the blow hit home. But I had no time to waste on pity, for at that instant Sophia entered, carrying a plain brown shift and wooden shoes.

"You may leave," I said to Simon. "You may not tell anyone what you have seen or done today."

Still silent, Simon bowed and went to the door. As Sophia had done earlier, he hesitated.

"Well?" I said, impatient to get on with it.

He looked at me, his round face pale. "Little Beetle—" he began.

"Stop calling me that!" I said.

He bowed once more. "Your Majesty—Princess Anna," he said, his voice quivering. "Think before you act. Remember Atreus. Remember Agamemnon."

"They are dead," I said. "I cannot change the past. But I can change the present. Now leave me before someone comes."

He stood for a moment longer, then went through the door. His footsteps receded down the corridor.

"Dress me!" I commanded Sophia. Her hands trembled as she did so and as she slid the heavy shoes onto my feet. I pulled the brown hood up over my head. "Hand me a mirror," I said. Sophia gave me a heavy bronze hand-mirror, and I examined myself. No one would know me in that disguise.

"Go to my mother's apartments," I instructed Sophia. "Tell her not to worry; tell her that by tonight we will be free."

Suddenly Sophia was on the floor, clutching my ankles with both her hands. "Princess," she was sobbing, "you can't do this! You will be caught, and tortured, and executed!"

"I will not be caught," I said. "I am much more intelligent than that—than that thing that calls itself the emperor. He will never find out."

"But you can't kill your own brother," she wailed. "It is against nature, and the laws of your God. Your God will punish you."

"So you expect his guardian angel to look out for him?" I asked. I would have laughed if I hadn't been in such haste. "Don't believe fairy stories, Sophia. Now let go of me."

She did not, and I had to bend down and loosen her hands from around my ankles. Leaving her crying on the floor, I slipped out the door and made my way down the corridor. Empty a few minutes before, it was now filled with servants, some going to their masters' and mistresses' bedrooms to robe them for the feast, others hastening to the kitchen and the banquet hall to make final preparations for that evening. I kept close to the wall, head down, trying to imitate the walk of the slaves. It proved easier than I had thought, since the wooden shoes made it difficult to take long steps. At the door leading out of the section of the palace where the bedchambers were, I saw two guards. One of them was the man who had been ordered to keep me out of the library. I was suddenly afraid he would recognize my face, even with the hood over my head. I pulled back into the shadows. After counting to one hundred, I looked out again. He was still there.

Time was running short. I had to enter the banquet hall before the guests arrived, so I decided to fetch Sophia and have her distract the guard while I slipped past. Retracing my steps, I returned to my bedchamber, but the room was empty. Now what? I pulled my courage together and went out into the corridor again.

Once more I made my way down the hall, and as I neared the guard, I saw he had been pressed into carrying a wooden bench into the kitchen. Taking advantage of his absence, I entered the banquet hall.

No one was about. Final preparations had been made,

and the servants must have been in the kitchen helping to get the food and drink in order. I walked as quietly as I could across the great hall. The tapestries glowed on the wall. The floor had been polished until it gleamed, and my wooden shoes slid on it until I was afraid I would fall. All was in readiness at the long tables, too. The bronze dishes, which I had last seen at my betrothal feast, were shining on the white cloths. Bread was already laid out, and artful arrangements of fruit on every table added color. The goblets were in place, and the servants had already poured wine in them. I felt weak with relief. No one would notice a few more drops of dark liquid in one of the cups. Most of the guests would be drinking from bronze cups, while silver was reserved for the imperial family. At the high table, a gold goblet encrusted with gems awaited the emperor.

I knew what I had to do. I moved toward the high table, flask in hand. Up a step to the throne I went—moving it back so that I could reach the table. My heart stopped at the squeak the wooden legs made on the marble floor. The smell of cedar rose to my nose, bringing hot tears to my eyes as I remembered how the scent used to cling about my father for hours after he left his seat. My knees felt weak, and I sat on the high seat of the throne to recover.

But I couldn't wait. Even as my head swam and I was afraid I would faint for the first time in my life, my hands were busy uncorking the flask. The smell that rose from it was not particularly strong, and I thought I could risk a fairly large dose without its being noticed. I tipped the flask, and the dark liquid splashed into the wine.

At that moment, a slight breeze reached me as the tapestry moved. I froze.

From behind the tapestry stepped John. With him was Anna Dalassena, her face so bright with triumph that I could not bear to look at it. John's face mirrored hers.

I could not move.

Another tapestry shook, and from behind it came four guards, swords drawn, faces grim.

"Seize her," said John.

As they moved in my direction, he added, his voice thick with gloating, "I hope you are comfortable. That is the last time you will ever sit on that throne."

CHAPTER
TWENTY-THREE

had never seen the dungeons before, but they were as I had always pictured them. The walls and floor were rough stone, and mildew grew over them in damp patches. A torch in the hall cast only a feeble light through a slit in the door, but I had no need to see anything. I supposed my mother was somewhere in the dungeon too, for whoever had betrayed me must have known that she was involved as well. I was certain I was going to be executed, and that my mother would be too. After all, what good would it do John to get rid of me if she was still alive?

I spent a long time—I'll never know how long exactly—in the cell. I wondered if the funeral feast had gone on as planned, or if my actions had disrupted it. I slept on the hard pallet on the floor, glad of the servant's woolen clothes I had on, since they were warmer than the thin silk I would have been wearing otherwise. I did not miss food, but I was growing increasingly thirsty, and wondered if John was going to let me die of neglect. I did not mind death—in fact, I embraced the idea. But I did mind wasting away. I had the right to die as a royal, by execution. The cold thought struck me that John would perhaps officially declare me illegitimate, and so unworthy of the executioner's steel.

As I considered this possibility, the door swung open, pushed by the burly arm of a guard. The guard stepped back to admit someone, and Sophia entered, carrying a tray.

I seized her arm, causing the tray to spill its contents.

"You!" I spat. "Traitor!"

"No, Princess—" said Sophia, trying to back away from me, but I held her tight.

"What did they offer you? Your freedom? So you could marry that man?"

"No, it wasn't me, I swear it!"

"Who else could it have been? No one else knew!"

"I don't know, I don't know—I admit that I did not want you to do it, that I would have stopped you if I could, but I didn't betray you. I didn't tell anyone!"

"If you didn't, who did?"

"I did," said a familiar voice. I dropped Sophia's arm and she spun around, so we were both facing the door. There, tears streaming down his face, stood Simon.

"No," I whispered. "No, it couldn't be you."

He stepped toward me, and stretched out a hand in my direction. I slapped it away before he could touch me.

"Why?" I said. "Why?"

He tried to speak, but was choked with tears. Finally, "Atreus," he said. "Agamemnon. I couldn't stand by and see that happen to you."

"And will you stand by and see what happens to me now?" I asked. "Will you come to the Purple Chamber and watch me blinded? Or will you hold my head in your lap as the executioner's sword slices through my neck?" He turned white.

"No, Princess..." he beseeched me. "This will not happen. He gave me his word—I made him swear on your father's soul—I told him that there was to be an attempt on his life but that I would not tell him who was behind it unless he swore neither to torture nor to execute the person involved. I told him that even under torture I would never betray who it was unless such assurance was made first. He didn't want to, but your grandmother realized the need for haste and forced him."

"And my mother?" I asked.

"No one knew she was involved until you were captured, when she went raving to the banquet hall, a drawn knife in her hand. She screamed that his life would be forfeit. The guards easily overpowered her. She is obviously mad; even the emperor recognizes it. He has agreed to send her to a convent in the mountains, where she will be looked after. Her servants are packing even now. She doesn't remember what has happened, and thinks she is going to join your father on campaign, the way she used to before you were born. She seems quite content."

That was some consolation. If she never regained her senses, she would never realize her situation. I was not so fortunate. When the guards had seized me, the flask had dropped from my hand and shattered on the floor, taking with it any chance I had to escape my fate.

And it was Simon's fault that I was here. I turned from him in loathing. "Go away," I said.

"Princess—Anna, my more-than-daughter—" he was sobbing now. I refused to look at him, and the guard ordered him out. The door closed, and I could finally allow myself to weep. I sat on the edge of the pallet, but no tears came. I was alone, for Sophia must have left when Simon did.

Several more days passed. I was finally allowed nourishment. I drank the water, but felt no desire for the bread and hard cheese that came on the tray. The days melted together. One of the guards was friendlier than the others, and told me that my mother had departed, locked in a carriage, laughing and having long, one-sided conversations with my father, with me, with her long-dead parents. He also told me that Simon had left the palace and no one knew where he was, although the emperor had instituted a search for him. I suspected that John had had him killed and ordered a search to cover his tracks. The thought made me feel a lead weight in my chest, although I tried to push it away, saying, "Traitor! Traitor!" to myself.

Finally, just as I had begun to think that I was going to finish my life in prison, a guard told me I had been ordered to the throne room. I was filthy and half starved. I knew that my miserable appearance would be a triumph for my brother but did not know what to do about it.

As I stood shakily on my feet, a knock came at the door. "You may enter," I said, knowing only one person knocked these days. It was Sophia. She was carrying a clean gown, which she helped me put on, and I sat on the edge of my cot as she washed and brushed my long hair, now bound back simply. I had no shoes, but cared little. At least I was neat and presentable.

I stepped out of the cell, leaning on Sophia's arm. The dim light of the one torch was painfully bright after weeks, I supposed, of near-total darkness. Four large guards accompanied us. I smiled inside at this ostentatious show of force, thinking that even if I had somewhere to go, I could not overpower one guard, much less four.

Sophia left me at the door and I stood in front of the throne while my brother pronounced sentence on me, our grandmother seated to his right. I was dismayed, but not surprised, to see Nicephorus Bryennius behind John. He avoided looking at me. But he need not have feared my hatred; I had no ill will toward him, and wished I could tell him so. He was loyal to his emperor, and after Simon's treachery I appreciated the quality of loyalty.

John was pronouncing my fate, and I pulled my attention to his words. To a Kecharitomene convent. In the mountains. It was fitting. And it was a good plan on his part. Far away, surrounded by religious women, I would find no allies to support me in any bid to regain the throne. It was all over, and for good.

He was speaking again, but suddenly Anna Dalassena stepped from behind the throne. Her face was distorted with anger.

"You have not listened to my command!" she said to John, ignoring me. "She deserves death."

John looked calmly into her face. "We do not do things that way anymore," he said. "Don't you remember what my father said when Anna talked about killing me for the first time? And in any case," he went on, "you cannot command me. *I* am emperor, not you."

It was as if a little cub had turned into a lion and bitten its trainer. Even in my misery, I enjoyed her look of disbelief as she struggled to speak. Now you see him for what he really is! I thought. You are rarely deceived in people, Grandmother, but this time he managed to conceal his true nature from you. Not the puppet you thought, but one who will do as he wants, despite what you tell him.

Finally she managed to sputter, "But—but—you wouldn't be emperor if it were not for me! I put you on that throne!"

"For which I thank you," he said, as though this were an ordinary conversation. "But I have no need of your services at this moment, and I command you to withdraw."

She stood stock-still, whether from shock or from a refusal to move, I do not know. John made a small motion with his hand, and a guard stepped forward. Surely she

190

would not suffer the indignity of being forced from the room. She must have had the same thought, for she began to leave.

"And Grandmother . . ." John called after her.

She looked over her shoulder.

"You forgot your bow," he said. She hesitated, then stiffly inclined her head, and strode from the room. I stifled a laugh. Not bad, Little Brother, I thought.

John turned his attention back to me and proceeded as though nothing had happened.

"Although you have shown yourself unworthy of any consideration, you once were my sister. I will allow you a certain measure of comfort above that of the nuns in the abbey. You may bring warm clothes and have a fire every day in the winter, and I will allow you one of your slaves."

"One slave?" I said. "Just one?"

He barked a short laugh. "Just one. You can learn to take care of yourself."

I ignored his jibe, although I had heard that he himself required three attendants just to get robed for an ordinary day. "Will this be one of your slaves that you allow me to take, or will she still belong to me?"

He waved his hand, clearly bored by the question. "What does it matter? Whichever you prefer."

His ministers nodded, and whispered to each other. I could hear one of them saying, "Such generosity!" Well, if he was generous, he was the victor, and could afford it.

"I choose the girl Sophia," I said.

"As you wish." He turned to one of his ministers and said, "See to it."

"Just one moment." I held up my hand. "It is clear that the slave Sophia is my property, to dispose of as I will?"

"Yes, yes," he said, impatience making his voice rise. "What do I care what you do with your maid?"

"Then hear me," I said. "I will go without servants to the convent. From this moment forth, the girl Sophia is to be free. She can never be claimed as anyone's slave."

I wheeled and strode out of the throne room, being careful not to make any motion that might be interpreted as a bow. I must have taken my guards by surprise, because they had to make little hopping strides so that they could catch up to me without breaking into an undignified run. As I passed Sophia, I saw her muddy brown eyes round and staring, her face shining as she returned my glance. I wondered why I had ever thought her ugly. I knew I would never see her again.

The journey to the convent took several days. As we passed through the city walls in the closed coach, I thought that surely now I would die; I had never been outside the walls before. Fields, farms, hills—they went past the window of the carriage. These sights were so strange to me that despite my gloom I kept the window-curtain pulled open so that I could look out, except when curious villagers tried to peer in at the deposed princess. Then I pulled the curtain closed and sat huddled in a corner.

The scenes outside the carriage window looked nothing like the bright illustrations I had seen in the psalm-book that Sophia had been so fond of, with their bright colors and busy figures. Most of what I saw was dreary. Rain fell

almost continuously, and at the inns where we s[...]
the stench of damp made me ill.

Eventually the flat plains turned into hills, and the hills into rocky mountains. There was no longer anyone to stare at me as I went past, so I kept the curtains open and watched the mountains as they grew nearer. But the closer we got, the less I liked the view. The mountains were hard and gray; they looked like cold shoulders turned against me. I pulled the curtains again and slept as much as I could to pass the time.

The horses labored climbing up the slopes, and on the way down the brakes were set against the wheels to prevent the beasts from being run over by the carriage. Up, up, up, and then down, down, down, until finally there were several days of more up than down.

On the afternoon of a particularly wet day, one of the grim-faced women assigned to travel with me said with distinct satisfaction, "There is your new home." I looked out and saw that we were pulling into the courtyard of a large gray building, made of stone and wood. The nuns who were gathering to see the newcomer wore habits of the same color, and any hair they had was covered by gray scarves. They blended in well with their surroundings. I descended stiffly from the carriage, and, followed by the two women carrying the possessions I had been allowed, I entered the convent.

And here I stay. Two years have passed since my arrival, and since I am only seventeen, many more years will pass before I move on to my next home, which will be the grave.

CHAPTER
TWENTY-FOUR

I t is cold here. Despite the concession of a fire each day, and the warm clothes allowed me, I never feel entirely warm. The only place where I can forget the cold is in the copying-room. Lately, after many weeks of irksome practicing under Sister Thekla, I have been given some actual documents to copy. They are private family papers, copied over for use in a lawsuit. It almost makes me laugh to see the petty matters in which these local lordlings are engaged. No Comnenus would lower himself to squabble over an inheritance, or over ownership of land. We would just take what was ours, or die in the attempt. Or be sent into exile.

In the months I have been writing here in my room, and enduring Sister

Thekla's tutelage in the copying-room, I have learned the names of some of the nuns. The little novice with the runny nose is Honoria. She was sent here as a tithe, she tells me. The peasants often vow one tenth of all they own to God, and since she was her parents' tenth child, they dedicated her as a nun. She is not unhappy with their choice, having grown up with the knowledge that this is what her life would be. Besides, she tells me, it is much more comfortable in the convent than in the farmhouse where she was born, and here no one beats her.

Others of the nuns have different reasons for being here. One, something of a celebrity in the small community, fled marriage with a man of superior rank to dedicate herself to Christ. The others speak of her with awe, as someone who had the courage to stand up to her father. Most were simply the younger daughters in a family with no means of providing a dowry for all the girls, and so had to come here for lack of any other way to live. A few, like Sister Thekla, are widows, and hold the novices, who have come without any knowledge of the world, in some contempt.

Mother Superior often summons me to her room, where there are comfortable chairs and a few rugs to keep the cold of early spring from one's feet. She is an affectionate person who treats all the sisters as her daughters. She calls me to her room on some pretext, but then keeps me there talking about history, about my mother, about the Franks who overran our country during the Crusade, about anything she can think of. She is more educated than the rest of them (except Sister Thekla), and I think her mind is as starved as mine for intelligent conversation.

Lately I have been attending some of the nuns' services. At first a few curious glances turned my way as I sat on my bench, but now they seem accustomed to my presence. I find their singing soothing. A few evenings ago they sang a hymn I did not remember having heard before, either in the palace or here. The melody was unremarkable, but the words were unusual. The next morning I asked Mother Superior what it had been. She called over Sister Theodora, the choir-mistress, and put my question to her.

"It was about Mary the Egyptian, whose feast-day it was yesterday," she answered. "If you like, Sister, you may borrow the hymnal and read it for yourself."

I nodded assent, and Theodora left, reappearing a few minutes later with her hymnal. She turned to a page marked "April I: Mary the Egyptian," and I read:

> *"You severed the temptations of the soul*
> *and the passions of the body*
> *with the sword of temperance;*
> *the crimes of the mind*
> *you choked with the silence of spiritual discipline,*
> *and with the streams of your tears*
> *you watered the entire desert,*
> *and made to grow in us the seeds of repentance:*
> *therefore we celebrate your memory, holy one."*

I admired the warlike imagery of the opening. I knew all about fighting my passions as though in a battle. At the bottom of the page was the name Kassia.

"Kassia," I said.

"A nun," Theodora replied. "She lived hundreds of years ago and wrote many hymns and verses."

"I have heard of her," I said. I asked no more questions, and Theodora, accustomed to the convent's rule against unnecessary conversation, volunteered no more information.

A few weeks ago, I noticed that there were fewer women than usual at the table one evening. Mother Superior noticed my inquiring look and after the meal was over she said to me, "I'm afraid that some of the sisters have been taken with an illness."

"What kind of illness?" I asked.

"They ache in all their joints and are unable to take nourishment," she replied.

"Are they feverish?" I asked.

"Yes, but not severely," she answered.

"May I see them?" I asked. She hesitated. "I have some skill in medicine," I told her, and after considering for a few minutes, she nodded and led me to the infirmary.

There, four nuns lay on little cots, three of them asleep, the fourth praying. I walked down the row, took their pulses, felt their foreheads for fever, and looked into the eyes and mouth of the one who was awake. Then I turned to the mother superior.

"It is nothing serious," I told her. "The important thing is for them to take in liquid. Not wine, but water, or if they can keep it on their stomachs, weak broth. Have them take a tiny sip, then wait a few minutes, and then take another. In that way their stomachs should be able to stay easy and not spew it all forth again."

The infirmary nun was listening eagerly, and when the mother nodded to her she bustled out of the room, I suppose to tell the kitchen nuns to prepare broth.

"They should continue to rest," I went on. "Do not bleed them, but make them stay in bed until they say they feel well, and then one day more. This fever returns easily and is more difficult to get rid of the second time."

"I thank you, daughter," she said.

In a few days, the four sisters were about their duties again, and a fifth who had taken ill recovered much faster than the others for having been started on my regimen earlier. The sisters started coming to me with their little ills (due mostly to boredom and inactivity), and I even started to treat the beggars who gathered in the courtyard seeking aid from the convent. The convent library had a few medical books, some of which were new to me, and I read them eagerly, immersing myself in study the way I had not done since the days when Simon and I would spend long hours in the library together. His round face appeared suddenly in my mind as I came upon a book he had once urged me to read, despite my reluctance. The book had looked dry, and was so old that the pages were brittle and hard to handle.

"Sometimes wisdom is hidden in an unattractive form," he had told me. I had rolled my eyes at the triteness of his words, and he had laughed. "And sometimes truth is hidden in clichés!" he had added. It was my turn to laugh, and I had picked up the book, studied it, and learned a great deal.

I felt a jolt when I realized that for the first time since

my exile I had thought of Simon without pain. Where was he now? I wondered. Was he thinking of me, too? Or had he been killed at my brother's orders?

Soon the villagers were looking on our convent as a kind of infirmary, and would bring me the ill and injured to receive aid. Yesterday, I had more than usual to deal with. Aside from the ordinary colds, fluxes, and scrapes and bruises, I had two wounds to treat. With the coming of spring, the farmers are working past their fatigue, and often make mistakes. I treated a deep gash from a scythe on a young man's leg, and set the arm of a boy who had fallen from a tree where he had been egg-hunting.

After I had received their thanks and their blessings, I watched the last of them depart through the gate. From the courtyard, I could see out to the fields. Spring was not yet in full flower, but the day was warm. On an impulse, I followed the peasants through the gate to stand on the grass immediately outside the convent walls. At first I felt giddy at not being enclosed by walls, but told myself not to be silly, that ordinary people stood out in the open every day. After a few minutes, I felt more relaxed, and looked down across the fields. What I saw delighted me. Far off, tiny figures were bending low, planting. Horses pulled plows, and the sound of birdsong reached my ears. The mother superior joined me, her hands tucked in her wide sleeves.

For a few minutes we stood in silence. Then I said impulsively, "It looks just like Sophia's favorite picture!"

"Who is Sophia?" she asked.

I didn't know how to answer. Finally, "A friend," I said.

"And what was her favorite picture?"

"An illustration in one of my mother's psalm-books," I explained. "It showed a spring day, with people planting, just like this. And over the city . . ." I stopped. I knew it was foolish, but before I could stop myself I had craned my neck to look back over the convent. Of course, there was no golden-winged angel hovering there, just as there had not been over the palace all those years before. But for a moment I had thought I would see one.

CHAPTER
TWENTY-FIVE

 returned to my room to find an unexpected pleasure: a letter from Maria. It was brief, and she was obviously writing cautiously. No doubt my brother had someone read letters before allowing them to be sent to me. She said she was well, and happily establishing herself in her new home several days' ride from Constantinople, where her husband's family resided. I missed her and could tell, even from her carefully worded sentences, that she must miss me too. I was somehow comforted by the thought that even if I had remained in the palace, I would hardly have seen her again, given her new home and my duties. So circumstances would have separated us, even if John had not.

I had barely finished the letter and folded it back up when Mother Superior sent a sister with word that I had a visitor. I was sure this was another patient, and was raising myself wearily when the nun said, "No, she's coming here," and stood back to admit a small figure wrapped in a brown cloak, the hood pulled up to keep the wearer from the cold of the spring evening. The woman pulled her hood off her head, and a pair of familiar brown eyes beamed at me.

Sophia. Sophia had come. I reached out for her hands, suddenly blinded by the tears stinging my eyes. For once I was glad I was no longer a princess and had no need to hide what I was feeling.

"I am glad to see you," I said.

"And I you," she answered.

"What brings you here?" I asked.

"After you—left," she said, and I smiled inwardly at the discretion of that neutral word, "Malik and I came to this region to live with Malik's brother. I have only just heard that a princess was living in the convent and knew it had to be you. The mother superior says you still have no maid, so I am here to offer you my services."

I looked around the meager room. Sophia's gaze followed mine, and surely she could see that there were no chests of silken robes to keep in order, no huge, roaring fire to stoke, no meals to arrange on a tray. I indicated my linen gown, and my simply dressed hair. She smiled, remembering, no doubt, how I used to complain at the hours it took to plait my hair into dozens of tiny braids and wind them in complicated patterns across my head.

"I have no need of a maid," I said. "But I do need a friend."

Before I knew it, Sophia's arms were around me and we were both laughing and crying at the same time. We stood so for a few moments, and then Sophia pulled away. "Have you heard the latest news from the palace?" she asked.

"No," I answered. "I hear nothing from there. What has happened?"

"Your grandmother," she said.

I turned away as a bitter taste rose in my mouth at the mention of that woman. "What about her? Has she finally died?" I asked when I could control my voice.

"No," said Sophia, "but I wager she would rather be dead. Your brother has divested her of all power. She stays only in the women's wing now and daily petitions him to return her to her position as chief counselor. But I understand that he refuses even to see her."

Well, that was something, anyway. Maybe there was hope for John. Although I doubted it.

Sophia suddenly smiled and reached for my hand. "Come—there is someone here who wants to meet you," she said.

"Who?" I asked.

"Come see," she replied, and pulled me through the doorway. We descended to the courtyard. It was the only place in the convent where men were allowed, and I was not surprised to see Malik, who was sitting on a box. He was holding a bundle in his arms. Sophia dropped my hand and took the bundle from her husband, passing it on to me.

Wrapped in the blanket was a tiny baby. It had Malik and Sophia's light-brown skin, and curly brown hair covered its head. It was a wonder to me. "A girl?" I asked.

"A girl," Sophia replied. "Our daughter, Anna."

For the second time that day my eyes clouded over, and a large tear splashed on the baby's face. Sophia reached for her. "Malik," she said, "the box."

Malik, silent as always, stood up and bowed shyly to me, motioning to the box he had been sitting on. I went to it and removed the top. There, arranged in neat bundles, were the papers I had been working on that last day in the library, along with my pens, bottles of fine ink, and many books. I picked one up. It was a chronicle of the Crusade, and would provide me with many of the names and dates I needed to complete my story of our father.

"How did you get these?" I asked Malik.

He looked at his wife, who nodded impatiently, saying, "Go on, husband; tell her yourself."

Malik cleared his throat and started, "When the emperor told me to destroy your books and papers, I put them in a box, preparatory to burning them. Forgive me, Princess, but I knew that my life would be forfeit if I disobeyed his command. I carried them outside and was preparing to light them, when . . ."

Again he looked at his wife, who once more said, "Go on, husband."

"When Simon—" I winced at the name, but wanted to hear the rest, so said nothing. "When Simon came bustling up, you know, that funny little run—" Again I winced, but motioned at him impatiently to continue.

"Well, he saw what I was doing and bade me stop, saying that he would do it himself, that when books are burned someone knowledgeable has to supervise to make sure that all the pages are consumed by the flame. I gladly left the task to him, and assumed that he had carried it out, until last year, when I was summoned to his deathbed."

"What?" I broke in. "Simon has died?"

Sophia took over. "Malik and I knew where in the city he had hidden himself," she said softly. "He was never the same since you were sent away, and when a sweating sickness went through the city last year he was felled by it and lived only a few hours. He knew he was going to die, and called Malik to him. I came too, to see if I could help."

"I wish—" I said, "I wish I could have told him—" I broke off, unable to say what I wanted. That only now did I realize how he had loved me. That I wished I could have told him that I loved him, that he had been my real father all along, and that I now realized he had not betrayed me, but saved me. Sophia took my hand.

"He knew," she said. "As he lay there, struggling to breathe, he said to me, 'If you ever see my little beetle again, tell her that I always loved her as a daughter. Remind her of Agamemnon and Iphigenia, of Atreus and Thyestes. Tell her I was keeping her from their fate.' " She stumbled over the unfamiliar names. "Do you know what he was talking about?"

I nodded, tears blurring my vision. Malik spoke up:

"And then Simon told me that he had never burned your things but had preserved them, knowing that if the emperor ever found them he would be tortured and executed. That was why he ran away before his room could be searched. He kept them carefully as a memory of you, and with his last breath he begged me to take them, and asked that if Fate ever brought us together, to give them to you. And here they are," he concluded simply, waving at the box.

And there they were, indeed. I pulled out the pages of fine bombazine, my fingers rejoicing in their feel after the rough parchment I had been touching that morning. I saw my own handwriting on the first page: *Alexiad*, it read. *The Deeds of His Majesty Emperor Alexius Comnenus.* At the bottom of the stack were many, many blank pages waiting to be filled.

I stood marveling, pulling out books, notes I had written, diaries I had kept of those days. With these I could write my history. I could tell the true story of Alexius, of my mother, of the great deeds of my family. I would mention Anna Dalassena and John, of course, but only when necessary. I would not allow them to tarnish the glory of the true Comneni, those whose name they had defamed.

As I examined my papers and books, the mother superior came bustling up to greet the newcomers, her usual welcoming smile on her lips.

I turned to her. "Mother," I said, "I would like you to meet my family."

AUTHOR'S NOTE

The real Anna Comnena lived from 1083 to 1153. Her father, Alexius I, came to power as emperor through his military might. When the Seljuk Turks threatened his empire, he asked Pope Urban II to lend him some soldiers to repulse them. The pope instead decided to ask all the forces of Christian Europe to band together to expel the Turks from Jerusalem, and the First Crusade was launched.

After her father's death, Anna and her mother tried to assassinate her brother John. They were caught and sent into separate exile. The convents were actually very comfortable, and scholars and philosophers gathered there. While in exile, Anna wrote *The Alexiad*, an eleven-book epic about the life of her father. Today this book is the major source of information about that period in Byzantium. Although Anna paints vivid word-portraits of many people, including her parents and Anna Dalassena, she mentions John only when strictly necessary. She never tells of her attempted assassination of him.

After the death of Alexius, John ascended to the throne and became one of the most beloved rulers of the Byzantine Empire. Although other historians agree with Anna's description of him as homely, he became known as John the Beautiful because of the good works he did for the people he ruled.

I have changed some of the facts of the story, mostly by compressing the period in which the events took place, eliminating some characters, and inventing others. There were more Comnenus brothers and sisters than just Anna, Maria, and John, for example, and Anna was not only engaged to Nicephorus Bryennius but actually married him, and they had several children together. Sophia and Simon are inventions, but I hope Anna had someone like them in her life.

Most people, including some historians, assume that women in the Middle Ages were even less literate than the men of the time. So it might seem surprising that a woman who lived in what some still call the Dark Ages was a respected historian, and that some medieval nuns spent their time and earned money for their convents by copying manuscripts. But although we will never know for sure, it appears that medieval women were about as literate as the men of the time, and educated nuns could certainly copy texts. Some women wrote their own books, as Anna Comnena did. Most of these women's works have been lost, and many books, not bearing the name of any author, are assumed for no real reason to have been written by men. It is to these forgotten women writers that this book is dedicated.

ABOUT
THE
AUTHOR

racy Barrett is the author of numerous
nonfiction books and short stories for
children. She has researched medieval
women writers, among them the Byzantine princess Anna Comnena, with a
grant from the National Endowment
for the Humanities. She lives in
Nashville with her husband and two
children and teaches at Vanderbilt Uni-
versity. *Anna of Byzantium* is her first
novel.